ALSO BY ROBERT POYTON

REMNANTS - FENLAND TALES OF
HORRORS & HAUNTINGS
INNSMOUTH ECHOES

THE DUNWICH TRILOGY
THE DUNWICH NIGHTMARE
THE DUNWICH CRISIS
THE DUNWICH LEGACY

THE WOLF WHO WOULD BE KING SERIES
WOLF IN SHADOWS
WOLF IN CHAINS
WOLF IN THE NORTH

ASSAULT TEAM 5 SERIES
NAYLOR'S WAR

INNSMOUTH ECHOES
ECHOES
ECHOES
ECHOES
ECHOES
ECHOES

www.innsmouthgold.com

THIS IS AN INNSMOUTH GOLD BOOK

ISBN: 978-1-78926-305-3   Paperback

Copyright@ 2018 R Poyton.
Originally published 2018

All rights reserved.
The moral right of the author has been asserted. No part of this book may+ be reproduced in any form or by any electronic or mechanical means including information storage and retrieval systems, without permission in writing from the author. The only exception is by a reviewer, who may quote short excerpts in a review.

This book is a work of fiction. Names, characters, places and incidents are either products of the author's imagination or used fictitiously. Any resemblance to actual events or locales or persons, living or dead, is entirely coincidental.

Cover design: Innsmouth Gold

Published by Cutting Edge on behalf of Innsmouth Gold.

www.innsmouthgold.com

CONTENTS

Foreword

The Confession of Brother Simon 9
(first printed in Remnants, 2017)

Innsmouth Sonnet 33

Full Fathom Five 35

Fear at the Fitz 41

Return to Providence 65

U-837 67

Innsmouth Acid 89

Shore Leave 103

Innsmouth Marina 115

The Watcher 155

Urbex 157

Do You Want to Live Forever? 187

Vostock 5 211

FOREWORD

I would imagine that after the mighty Cthulhu, one of the names most associated with iconic horror author HP Lovecraft is Innsmouth. His tale *The Shadow Over Innsmouth,* set in the decaying New England seaport , regularly tops the lists of aficionado's favourite HPL tales.

Like most, I believed Innsmouth to be purely a product of HPL's fertile imagination, originating, perhaps, from one of those vivid dreams that so often informed his work. Imagine my surprise, then, when the effects of a former long-lost Great Aunt recently came into my possession, following her passing away at the age of 108.

Included with the usual family documents and personal effects, was a somewhat aged and battered tin box. Locked, yet there was no key to be found, search as I may amongst my Great Aunt's meagre possessions. And so the box lay dormant, tucked away at the back of the wardrobe for many weeks, while my work took me on numerous trips overseas. It was only after my return, one cold January night, that I came across the box again. Truth be told, I had forgotten its very existence.

Now intrigued, I removed the box and placed it on my desk. Closer scrutiny revealed no markings and nothing beyond a simple lock between me and the mystery within. Putting down my whisky, I found and straightened a paper clip from the drawer and set to work on the lock. Within a minute, there was a satisfying click and I opened the lid to look inside.

I wish to God I hadn't. Oh, what dark nightmares have plagued me since I tipped the contents of that cursed container onto my desk. For what tumbled forth was a sheaf of yellowed notes wrapped around a bundle of photographs, many of them decades old and faded. Each photo had writing on the back, in the hand of my Great Aunt, giving name, date and place of the subject. Each was a family member, part of my own lineage. And some of them came from Innsmouth!

Leafing through the papers gave me inspiration for this collection, spanning as it does many times and places... things past and things yet to come. I also print some of those photos here so that you may see the family line from whence such tales have sprung. Perhaps you will also understand, and have some sympathy for, my terrible predicament.

On the positive side, those notes spurred me to gather together these tales of people and places. Family is so important, don't you think? For, after all, are any of us more than the sum of our previous generations?

However... I look less and less in the mirror these days. Most of my time is spent at my desk, curtains drawn against the hurtful sunlight, repeatedly referring to my Great Aunt's papers, delving deeper into my family history. Make of this collection what you will but take heed that sometimes the past is a country best left unexplored. And remember... Innsmouth is not just a place, it's a state of mind.

THE CONFESSION OF BROTHER SIMON

Tower Bruer Templar Preceptory, 29th October 1216

Abbot Thomas nodded to the gatekeeper who had let him into the courtyard and made his way swiftly to the preceptory. The journey from Kirkstead had been somewhat hurried and uncomfortable but Abbot William's message had urged all possible haste, as well as discretion. All Thomas knew was that he was to perform absolution for a person here at Tower Bruer. Once inside, he was led quickly into a side room and given some plain, but welcome, victuals. The room was small, lit by a few candles, furnished only with a table and two chairs. After a short time a young man came in to clear away the plate and cutlery. Almost as soon as he had left, a tall figure, dressed in white monk's robes, entered and sat on the plain chair opposite. Thomas could see little of the person's face, save something of the chin. The head remained bowed, hands held together within the long sleeves.

"Father forgive me, for I have sinned. I would make my confession," came a whispering but steady voice from the cowl.

"But of course Brother. Where would you like to begin?" The Abbot leaned forward attentively.

"By first saying, Abbot, that I am no Brother. I am not a monk, I am a Templar Knight. Forgive the deception, but it proved necessary for my task."

"And this task, the reason for this deception, it was some undertaking of great import my son?"

"Indeed it was Father - it was in order to murder King John!"

Croyland Abbey, 8th October 1216

As he nudged the pony across the narrow bridge and into the marketplace, Abbot William noticed at once the two burley, cowled figures ahead who moved towards him. While outwardly dressed as monks, it was clear they bore weapons and armour beneath the plain robes.

"Abbot William? I'm... Brother Simon." The lead figure took the pony's reins, while the other glanced about. "I've been asked to meet you and take you into the abbey."

"Very well... Brother. Please lead on." William nodded and allowed himself to be led through the small market and into the grounds of the abbey. Dismounting and handing his horse to a young monk, William followed the two figures through an archway and along a short corridor, which ended in a stout wooden door. Brother Simon knocked sharply and the door opened a fraction. After a short pause, it was opened fully and William was ushered into the room, followed by Brother Simon. The other "monk" took up position outside the door.

"Ah Abbot William, such a pleasure to see you again!" A grey haired, elderly monk rose to greet William, black robes contrasting with his own white. He advanced, grasping William's hands. Elderly perhaps, but the grip and twinkle in the eye showed no sign of age or infirmity.

"Abbot Geoffrey," William smiled. "I see the years have been kind to you! Why the last time we met must have been in Cyprus, do you reme-"

"Harrumph!" coughed a corpulent figure seated at the room's large table. "Much as I enjoy hearing old tales of derring-do, might I remind you that we are here for important issues and that this meeting is extremely hazardous to all!"

"Apologies Milord," Geoffrey made a shallow bow. "You must forgive an old soldier. Allow me to introduce Abbot William of Swineshead Abbey."

William stepped forward and bowed his head. Abbot Geoffrey gestured to each in turn, beginning with the corpulent nobleman.

"Robert de Gresely, Baron of Manchester. Abbot Adam of Croxton." This to a tall, thin monk. "Sir Simon of the Templar order," this to the cowled figure who had brought William in. "Hugh Bigod," a fresh faced young man half rose and bowed. "And his father, Sir Roger Bigod."

This towards the lean figure dressed in fine hose leant against the narrow window ledge at the far end of the room. This man turned and bowed slightly to William, then stepped forward to the head of the table to address the conspirators.

"Let us begin, gentlemen. Firstly, I'm sure I need not remind you that no word of what passes here today shall leave this room, many of us have already suffered enough at the King's hand. We wish to put an end to such suffering and tyranny. I'm sure we all have our own reasons for wishing the King were....

gone"

"I'll say," huffed de Gresely. "He's already threatened to increase the price of bread forty fold in order to fill his tax coffers! Outrageous!"

"Indeed," agreed Abbot Geoffrey. "And let us not forget what he has already done. Both Peterborough and our own Abbey here at Croyland were cruelly sacked by the tyrant, even the sacred vessels were carried off!"

"The Guthlac Roll?" interjected Abbot Adam.

"We were fortunate to save that, by the grace of God," replied Geoffrey. "The looters were more inclined to earthly rather than spiritual treasures."

"Many local estates have suffered in similar fashion." spoke the young Hugh. "Raids, punitive measures, taxation. It really is beyond the pale!"

"I understand the King is not even beyond base blackmail concerning more delicate matters?" Geoffrey inclined his head towards the reddening Adam, who busied himself with the large bag at his feet. Few people knew of his dalliance with a certain noblewoman of Croxton Kerrial.

"In any case," continued Sir Roger, "Dauphin Louis has landed in Kent and is moving towards London. King Alexander once again moves south from Scotland. If we make our play correctly, we will have the support of much of the nobility. However, if the King is very obviously murdered, then who knows how the people will react? We know not where Marshall will stand, nor any of those other powerful men who currently waver. Father Adam, you have some thoughts on this?"

Adam brought forth a collection of vials and jars from his bag.

"I have some experience with herbal matters. Here are a range of substances which will, if ingested, bring about death. There are two difficulties, though. The first is in administering such a poison to the King. Each of these has a strong taste, which would be difficult to mask, for one thing. And let us not forget that the King is never without his taster! Another problem is that the effects of these herbs are widely known. Belladonna, hemlock, it would be obvious to even a half-trained eye that the King has been poisoned. We can only wonder what repercussions may fall on those in close proximity to the King at the time."

"Why not more direct means?" the young Hugh stood, grasping the hilt of his dagger. "Get in close and finish it!"

"You forget Sir Savaric, the King's bodyguard," responded Simon. "An armed person would not get within ten feet of the King, especially given his current state of mind. And if they did succeed, that brute Savaric would immediately cut then down!"

"A person in disguise may be able to get close." Geoffrey arched his eyebrows, motioning to Simon's robes.

"True, but it is still a mission whose outcome would be certain death. We could not expect anyone to sacrifice themselves so, however just the cause," said Sir Roger.

"Perhaps an ambush?" suggested de Gresely. "We know the King may well travel across the Wash from Lynn, surely this is an opportunity for a small band of brave men to waylay him en route? There will be no-one to see, the King might be assumed to have been lost in the marsh, Lord knows the area is treacherous enough!"

"An attack in the marshes? Impossible!" replied Sir Roger. "There is no concealment for ambush. Furthermore, the tracks only allow single file for horses and to step off the track in armour is to invite certain death in the mud. The area will be as dangerous to us as to the King's men. Consider also, the King will have a strong force with him to guard his train. Besides we cannot be sure the King will travel with the baggage train, he may take some other route that will provide the luxury more befitting his station."

"We are at impasse then gentlemen," sighed Adam. "Will no-one rid us of this troublesome King?"

The room lapsed into thoughtful silence. William sat pondering, his face troubled, then he spoke up.

"There is another way," he ventured. "But it is fraught with peril and may even endanger our immortal souls."

"Explain," asked Sir Roger. "A this stage I would sign a deal with the Devil himself! Forgive me Father," he hastily added noting Geoffrey's disapproving scowl.

"I was born and raised in a small village not far from here," William told them. "Lutton, a remote hamlet on the coast. There was a local woman living out away from the rest of us; she was called Mother by the locals. There were many rumours and legends about her. I saw her once, when I was a small boy. The catch had been bad that season, we faced the prospect of a hungry winter, so the village elders approached Mother and asked her to perform a certain ritual. This is an old country, gentlemen; before the coming of the Word of Our Lord there were many old ways practiced here. Some say there are... others... those who were here before us, who can be turned to for help. So it was that one day at the water's edge, Mother carried out her pagan ritual. My father took me home early, so I saw very little. True to Mother's word, the catch increased the next day and the following day. In fact, we had an overabundance for many weeks after."

"Well, that's all well and good," interrupted de Gresely. "But how do witches by the sea help our predicament?"

"By this, Milord. The witch, as you call her, may have some method of striking at the King, many spoke of the curses she used against enemies. If she has access to such powers, then mayhap she can persuaded to help us. Assuming she still lives, of course; she looked old when I was a boy, though many village elders spoke of her being there when they were but children themselves."

"Good God, have we come to this," asked Geoffrey. "Shall we turn to pagan devils to do our work?"

"Some might say it is already the Devil's work," said Simon. "What matter the instrument if the intent be good? Do we condemn the sword for cutting down the disbeliever? The rope for hanging the traitor?"

"*Put not your trust in princes, nor in the son of man....*" quoted Geoffrey , placing his head in his hands. "Very well. Speak to your witch, Brother William, then let us reconvene and make further decision."

The group nodded assent and one by one the conspirators left, furtive and cloaked.

Lutton, The Wash, three days later

Abbot William nudged the donkey along the narrow track. Tall reeds obscured the view to each side and did something to protect him from the chill breeze blowing in off the sea. He had spent the night at Sutton St Mary's, though had said nothing of his mission to the clergy there. As far as anyone was concerned, he was merely revisiting his boyhood home and family.

The donkey was slow but steady - and steady counted for a lot in this region. A horse that skittered due to a marsh fowl being put up may well run straight into the water, or worse, the mud. Although it was barely mid-morning a low mist already moved across the path. The settlement of Lutton shortly came into view, clinging, as it did between the marsh on one side and the sea on the other.

Leaving his donkey in the care of the small tavern, William set off along the beach. Winding his way between fishermen busy at their small boats, he made for the far end of the strand. There he found the track he remembered from his youth, one that as children they dared each other to run along, the one that led to Mother's house. William strode on and within seconds, village, fishermen and sea disappeared from view. He found himself winding deeper and deeper into the marshes, midges and other insects swarming around him. The monk felt uncomfortably hot and sticky despite the chill autumn breeze; the atmosphere grew oppressive, there was a dank smell in the air. Strange bird cries sounded every now and then, though William never saw a sign of any bird.

William was almost ready to give up, thinking Mother was no longer alive, when the track opened into a small clearing. A handful of tumbledown shacks ringed the space, patchwork constructions of mud, wattle and old boat timbers. In the centre of the clearing a crudely carved stone pillar thrust skyward.

Nothing moved. William stepped closer to the central stone; it was larger than a man, though quite thin. He made out carvings as he approached it, curious figures, squat, with distorted features. Other lines suggested some form of script, though as William stared at them they seemed to writhe and move slightly. He felt the pull of something beyond his understanding, as though he stood on the gulf of a precipice, where up was down and if he pitched forward he would not fall, but rise... rise through dark, green depths, up towards the distant light.... a light in which were outlined the silhouettes of strange creatures swimming above him... beckoning.

"Don't get too close - you may not come back!"

William jerked back, he had gotten much closer to the stone than he thought. He spun round to see a figure framed in the dark doorway of the largest hut. Mother. She was a short yet stocky figure, with a hint of hidden strength in her posture and movement. She showed no signs of age or infirmity. Shapeless rags concealed much of her and, in many ways, William was grateful for it.

Long, lank hair framed a squat, misshapen face. Large, bulbous eyes surveyed him; they seemed to have faint luminous glow in the half light of the shack. A stubby nose in the centre, underlined by a curiously wide mouth, thick lips curled up at one edge in amusement. Mother lifted a flabby, mottled arm and beckoned. "Enter, priest!"

William walked into the hut, though it took some willpower to do so. He felt the touch of unseen eyes from the other shacks.

"Sit!" Mother beckoned to a stool beside a low table. William sat. With an effort he kept his gaze forward and down - he had glimpses of things hanging in the hut that he had no wish to examine closely.

"Speak!" Mother sat opposite him.

"I seek assistance in a difficult task. A means to remove

someone that will leave no obvious trace. This person is important and we must take all means in order to-"

"I know of whom you speak," hissed Mother. "I hear all in these parts, especially of those who bring fire and sword into the Fen!"

"Then you sympathise with our cause? You will help rid us of the tyrant?"

Mother cackled, a curious bubbling, wheezing sound. William blanched as her foul breath rode over him.

"Your cause? Your cause? What is your cause to me? You are here and gone quicker than the tide, your lives are nothing more than a wave upon the ocean. Those you call Kings are but beggars before the true rulers, swine digging in the mud. Your so-called Kings will come and go and the Old Ones will still remain!"

"What is this blasphemy you speak, our Church and King rule this land, now and forever!" William protested. Mother laughed once more.

"Ah, but the future! The future, priest. I have seen it in my dreams! Your abbeys and grand buildings will be ruins... bony fingers pointing to the sky. Your grand knights will burn! Fire and pestilence will sweep your lands, your Kings will be gone, executed by their own kind. And you speak to me of your cause?"

Mother arose, smiting the table with a heavy fist. Unblinking she leaned towards him, a strange gleam playing in her eyes. "And yet... I shall give you what you require... though there is a price."

"Name it and let me begone from this place," stammered William.

"Gold. Jewels. Such trifles can be useful to my kind. The reasons need not concern you."

"The King has gold with him, carried in a baggage train. "

"Then we will take the King's gold."

"But there will be archers, men-at-arms, soldiers, you have none of these here."

Mother sat down and laughed again. "How ignorant you are. Bring word of the train's whereabouts and the rest shall be arranged."

"Very well.... I agree. Now, can you provide what we need?"

Mother turned and reached into a dark corner of the hut, then placed a small vial on the table.

"This is what you seek. It is a draught that assists with The Change. In large enough doses it will bring a fast and ruinous adjustment to the human body, more than a human can cope with. The body will bloat, the insides will become... different. It will look like no poison known to man."

"Change? What is this change of which you speak?"

Mother cackled again. "You think you are made in your God's image? You are made in their image.... or at least from the same clay! You carry their seed within you!"

"They? Who are they?"

"The Ones who were here before and will be here long after your kind is gone. For the oceans will rise again! Your kind may tame the seas for a time but it will be like holding back the waves with sand. All this will again be their domain!"

William shuddered and grabbed the vial. With the speed of a snake, Mother grasped his wrist, in a surprisingly strong grip. "Would you like me to show you? There are those here undergoing the Change... those born of them! "

Mother drew closer, mocking William's look of horror. "Oh yes priest, for you see your kind has some uses... as breeding stock!"

With a wrench William pulled himself free and ran from the hut. The mocking laughter of Mother followed him as he leant against the rough wall of the hut opposite, trying to compose himself.

A sound made him turn, something moved inside the hut. Through gaps in the wall he caught sight of something large, a greyish bulk. Then a large blank eye appeared at the gap, like a milky pearl. There was a loud croak as the thing banged on the hut wall, as though seeking to break through to the monk. William took to his heels, running back to the beach as though he were a young man again. Not until he reached the village did he stop, gasping for breath and praying fervently.

Lynn, two days later

Geoffrey de Serland raised his eyebrows to his brother Raymond as they approached the King's chamber. From inside, they could hear the King's raised voice.

"I said wine you fool, bring me wine, not this horse piss!" The sound of a goblet being hurled against the wall was followed by the door opening and a flustered serving lad leaving the room at great speed.

The two knights entered. King John sat a table, chewing on a joint of meat. As was common these days, he seemed in foul temper. News of the continuing rebellion had just reached him and lent even greater urgency to his plans.

"You, out!" He gestured with the beef bone to a tearful

maid who clasped the torn material of her blouse with white-knuckled hands. The wench fled and the King gestured to his bodyguards to be seated.

"Once it is assembled, I'm sending you two with the baggage train across the Wash. The sooner we get everything to Lincoln the better. Savaric and a small group will accompany me. We will travel around the marshes, I'll not spend another day in this hellhole, this damp plays havoc with my joints!"

"The baggage train across the marshes sire, is that wise?" ventured Raymond.

"Tis a faster route," explained the King. "Local guides have been arranged, it will save days of travel and there will be no chance of those damned rebels getting their hand on my treasures!" The last was shouted and led King John into a coughing fit. "It is decided! Now, where is that boy with the dammed wine!"

Swineshead Abbey, the next day

"Good tidings, my fellows," Abbot Geoffrey addressed the group. "Not only has Brother William our required... medicine... but we have also received news that the King will be travelling separately from his retinue and baggage train. Furthermore, he plans to rest here overnight before moving onto Lincoln."

"We have our chance then!" Exclaimed de Gresely. "Within these walls we can get close to the tyrant!"

"But it still begs the question," pointed out Adam. "How do we administer the dose?"

"I will do it," spoke Simon. "It would not be meet to ask

one of the Brothers to do it. I am a soldier, it is my duty to protect my order, by any means necessary. I will disguise myself as a monk and serve the tyrant his last drink."

"And the poison - it will leave no trace?" asked Hugh.

"Oh there will be some marked effects but they will appear to be caused by disease rather than poison," replied William. "In any case, we hope that Brother Adam will be on hand tend to the body as soon as possible and do his best to disguise anything questionable."

"It is decided then," said Sir Roger. "Let us pray for success gentlemen!"

"And also for our souls," added Abbot Geoffrey. "Abbot William, I would ask you give absolution to Simon before the deed. He does an evil thing for a good cause and I would have no stain on his soul because of it!"

Abbot William nodded his assent and guided the young Templar knight into the chapel.

Walpole Cross Keys, the next day

Geoffrey de Serland counted the wagons as they passed him, rumbling through the narrow street. His brother Raymond was positioned at the head of the column, alongside the guide, followed by a small group of men-at-arms. Archers were positioned at intervals along the wagons and Geoffrey was to bring up the rear with another group of men-at-arms.

"That's the lot, sir!" said one of the men-at-arms.

"Alright John, I'll ride with you at the back if you think an old bastard like me can keep up."

The grizzled soldier chuckled and spat into the straw at

his feet. "Reckon the quicker we get across these marshes the better, looks like fog coming in already!"

The long train set out along the narrow track that led from the town into the marshes. The tread of hooves, the jingle of harness and the low murmur of men were deadened by the surrounding mists. A light drizzle began to fall. Each man spoke quietly to his nearest companion, or remained wrapped in his own thoughts.

At the head of the column, Raymond led his horse by the bridle, keeping close to the guide. The guide was a strange, stunted looking character but he seemed assured in his step and made no hesitation when coming to forks and branches in the track. The path was narrow and rose above the surrounding marsh in most places. Vegetation was sparse and the dark, shiny mud and brackish water lay on every side as far as the eye could see. As they progressed the fog became thicker still, until Raymond could see scarce ten feet in any direction.

It was close to midday, yet little could be seen of the sun save a pale hazy glow overhead. Raymond's horse began to wicker and whine, pulling on the bridle as he led the beast. He heard the same sound from the horses behind him and turned to see if there was any cause for the disturbance. When he turned back, the guide had vanished! Raymond cursed under his breath - what treachery was this? There was sudden movement in the mud and water around them. Raymond drew his sword, roaring "To arms! To arms!" and looked around in vain for an enemy.

The alarm travelled down the column to the rearguard. Geoffrey turned to John beside him - but the old soldier was no longer there, he had gone! Then shapes born of nightmare hove into view. On all sides, figures rose from the mud and water. Broadly man-like in size and outline, but with features that were in no way human... toad-like faces, unblinking fish eyes... what seemed like gills along the neck. The creatures were greyish green in colour, with large webbed talons. With a hideous croaking they fell on the baggage train. Sharp claws wreaked havoc amongst the surprised men, blood sprayed brightly into the air, men cried out in fear and pain.

At the head of the column Raymond let out a roar as his horse was dragged screaming by two of the creatures backwards into the water. Within seconds the stallion was up to its shoulders in the glutinous mud as the devils tore at it . The young knight put all his power into an overhead blow, bringing his sword down the shoulder of the nearest creature. The impact shocked up his arm and with dismay he saw that he had barely made any mark on the beast's tough hide. The creature back-swiped him and Raymond fell heavily to the floor, stunned.

He struggled to his knees, nose pouring blood, as the scene of carnage unfolded around him. The wagon drivers died first, being dragged down and eviscerated in the mud, their gore splashing red in the grey gloom. Small knots of men-at-arms stood shoulder to shoulder and attempted to fight the creatures. They were either clawed to pieces, despite their armour, or dragged screaming off the path and into the sucking mud, where they floundered and drowned. Horses and men cried out in their agonies, the creatures continued their hideous croaking and the terrible slaughter continued.

Within a matter of minutes, neither man nor horse was left alive. Bodies were pulled off of the path and hurled out into the marsh, or worse, consumed. Wagons were ripped apart, chests and bags containing the King's treasures carried off by the creatures into the fog, never to be seen again by human eyes.

Swineshead Abbey two days later

The King was in an even fouler temper. There was still no word of the baggage train, or any of the retinue accompanying it. He had spent the previous day at Wisbech, where the train was due to appear. Now he sat in the abbey refectory, brooding. The grim figure of his bodyguard, Sir Savaric de Mauleon, loomed behind him, always close at hand.

"God's wounds can no-one tell me what is going on?" The assembled monks flinched at the King's outburst.

"Our messengers have returned milord," Abbot William ventured. "None have seen any sight of the train after it left Lynn. There are few ways in and out of the marshes; we fear the whole train may have been lost. It is a very treacherous place."

"Treacherous? Treacherous? You speak to me of treachery, you mealy mouthed priests! Don't think I am ignorant of your conniving, your plotting, you're lucky I don't have you all put to death!"

At this Savaric's hand moved to the hilt of his broadsword. Abbot William swallowed hard.

"I assure Milord, we have only his best interests at heart."

"Bring me food and drink and plenty of it! And that pretty little wench I saw on the way in? Send her to my chambers later!"

"But milord that is Sister Judith - not only is she my own sister, but she is a Bride of Christ!" William looked horrified but the King was relentless in the pursuit of his passions.

"Do you dare defy me, monk? Deliver her to my chamber this night, or your head will be on a spike over your main gate, do you understand? Drink, man! Food!"

Abbot William rushed from the room to the kitchens. Simon was there waiting, dressed in the white robes of the order.

"It is time," the Abbot said to the young Templar.

"I'm ready father," answered Simon pouring Mother's potion into a large goblet of cider. "And Gold help us all."

The food was carried in on platters and Simon followed with the goblet. The food was laid out in front of the King.

"About time!" he shouted. Simon approached with the goblet and, bowing his head, proffered it to the King.

"Hmmm..." the King glanced up at the disguised Templar, then at the goblet. "Taste it!"

"Pardon milord?" Simon asked in a querulous voice.

"You heard me... taste it! My taster is with the train.... you are here. So taste it!"

Simon looked around the room. Abbot William stood still as a statue, perhaps offering some internal prayer. Savaric's hand once again moved to his sword hilt. Simon lifted the jewelled goblet to his lips and took a draught. There was no indication in taste of the presence of the witch's potion. Simon lowered the goblet, all eyes were on him. For what seemed like an eternity the King said nothing. Then he snatched the goblet out of Simon's hand.

"On your way, boy!" he snarled, before taking a deep draught of the cider. Simon, afraid that his legs would buckle under him, bowed and slowly walked out of the chamber. The Abbot followed, clutching the young man's arm as he leaned against the wall in the corridor and exhaled heavily.

"I confess father, I have faced fanatical men in battle but nothing filled me with as much fear as that moment!"

"You did well my son. Now, we just have to wait. In the meantime I will advise Sister Judith to leave immediately, in case our plans go awry."

It was an hour later, after the King had retired to his private chamber, that there was first indication of success. Savaric appeared, summoning the Abbot to the King's side. When the Abbot entered the chamber, the King was lying on the bed in considerable distress. His face was grey and clammy, his breath foul.

"Have you a physician here Abbot?" the bodyguard asked? William nodded and sent for one of the monks. He arrived and set about examining the King, who complained vociferously at every prod and turn.

"I fear the King has a fever and some ailment of the digestion," the monk reported. "I suggest he rest here for the night."

"Rest be dammed," the King hissed through clenched lips. "I must away to Lincoln!" He attempted to rise, then clutching his stomach fell back on the bed.

"If I might suggest Milord, rest here the night, then travel on to Lincoln tomorrow?" Abbot William offered. The King nodded and waved a hand in dismissal. Abbot William exited the room, going straight to see Simon.

"It has worked, the potion has taken hold! According to Mother it will take a day or two to do its work. Well done, Simon, you may have saved us all. Now, I suggest you leave quickly, lest any suspicions be aroused and we are questioned."

Simon nodded. "I shall return to the preceptory at Temple Bruer and await further news."

The next morning the King's entourage prepared to leave Swineshead Abbey. The King was carried, slumped between two courtiers and placed into his carriage. Without a glance at the Abbot and assembled monks, he waved the group on, his bodyguard flanking him on a great charger. It was the last they ever saw of the King.

Tower Bruer Templar Preceptory, 29th October 1216

"I'm sure you know the rest, Father Thomas," the cowled figure concluded. "The King arrived at Lincoln castle, then died the next day. Word was put out that his bowels had burst asunder in order to discourage viewing of the corpse. Of course, we had made sure that Abbot Adam was in place to attend to the body. The few servants with the King had already fled it seemed, after looting his belongings, the bodyguard was gone too. Adam prepared the body as best he could, though by all accounts there had been considerable changes to the Kings appearance. That may have also worked in our favour, as those who did see the body were not overly keen to closely examine a diseased corpse. "

The man paused and let out a sigh. "In any case, Brother Adam did his best and the King's corpse was packed and sent down to London for burial. None has come forward to challenge anything; as far as all are concerned the King died of some natural malady. The way is now clear for the Dauphin, let the dice fall where they may."

The hooded figure paused and sat back, as if some load had been lifted from him.

"I understand my son." Thomas assured him. "I am sure we are all thankful to be rid of the tyrant." Then he asked the question that was to haunt him for the rest of his days.

"But one thing puzzles me. You recounted in your tale how Abbot William granted you absolution for the deed you were about to do. Why now do you seek absolution again for that deed?"

The figure opposite him laughed, an unpleasant, croaking sound that carried no humour in it.

"Ah, well no.. you see Father I don't seek absolution for what I have done. I seek absolution for what I am going to do.... and what I am going to become. For I drank of the potion, Father. Not a great amount, but I drank of it nonetheless."

"I don't understand, surely the potion was fatal only in large doses?"

"Fatal yes. But in smaller doses, it brings about change, and already there have been changes. They are quickening too. So you see, Father, I can no longer remain here, I can no longer be part of this Order. You must pray for what little remains of my soul Father, for shortly I shall be with *them*. I shall be of them and at one with them. I understand now where we are from. The horror is, Father, that while part of me abhors this change another part of me welcomes it. In fact, it revels in it. I see you look confused. Then, Father, if words will not suffice, perhaps sight will..."

With that the figure lifted its hands to the cowl. The sleeves of the robe fell a little, exposing grey, rough-skinned arms. Simon pulled back the hood and Thomas screamed, as he looked into the ocean-spawned features of a man that was no longer a man.

INNSMOUTH SONNET

Shall I compare thee to a winter's day?
Thou art more lovely and more terrible:
Rough winds do stir the waves of Innsmouth Bay,
And drive us down to depths more bearable:
For too hot the cursed eye of heaven shines,
Though soon will his golden face be dimm'd
When certain stars in certain ways align,
And rises Cthulhu, savage, tentacled and winged:
But thy eternal darkness shall not fade
Nor lose possession of that fear thou insp're;
Nor shall thou wander in Death's impotent shade
But in eternal glory dwell in Yha-nthlir.
So long as Dagon lives or eyes can see,
So long live you and this gives life to me.

INNSMOUTH ECHOES

FULL FATHOM FIVE

D^{*ing dong bell*}

It is my own fault, of course. I shouldn't read just before going to sleep. Those old stories, they excite the imagination so. And now alone in the house, the old house, right here on the cliff tops, those crumbling cliff tops. Beyond, only the white-tipped waves, dark and whispering in the moonless night, hissing along the shore. Then, that other sound...

Ding dong bell

Of all the authors to read, I chose the Bard. Not *Macbeth*, no, too bloody. *Midsummer Night's Dream*? Too fey. *Othello*? Most definitely not, too soon since the loss of my beloved Annabelle. *The Tempest*, then; the stranded Prince, the monster and the sea. The eternal sea. And it is from the sea I hear that sound in my dreams...

Ding dong bell

It is hard to imagine that even in Shakespeare's time those bells were no longer on land. The great storm, it is told, swept them away, our own mighty tempest that drowned the town of Dunwich centuries ago. Proud, Christian bells that once stood in mighty towers are now deep beneath the waves. Yet still they ring...

Ding dong bell

What crime did the people of that town commit, I wonder? What foul deed deserved such punishment? For since that time little has remained of a once bustling port, save a crumbling abbey, one last church and a few houses. The only trade now a handful of dour and melancholy fishermen dragging a living from the impassive sea. Every year the cliffs crumble a little more, every year the implacable sands of time trickle away. The sea seems content to devour Dunwich piece by slow piece now, appeased perhaps by its gluttonous actions of old. Few houses remain between cliffs and windswept heath. My own is one such, for two years a happy home where I dwelt with my bride. Annabelle, sweet Annabelle, why did you leave me?

Ding dong bell

Those bells, tolling in the deep. I believe I heard them once as a child, on the night my father passed away. But you know how children are prone to wild imaginations. Since then, in all those years, not a sound. It must be the book, putting ideas into my head. A childish dream, a nightmare and I am now in that waking state where dream echoes into reality, that soft borderland that lies between the realms of Morpheus and the mundane. And yet... I hear them still and am now fully awake. Distant but clear, sonorous and low.

Ding dong bell

Lighting a candle I move to the window to draw back the shutter and peer into the dark. The pale reflection of my own face stares back at me from the glass. Beyond, only the pitch black of night. And there, that faint tolling once more. My old coat hangs on the back of the door, I wrap myself in it, use the candle to light a lantern, and step out of the old house. Presently I carefully tread the short path that leads along the cliff top. The hissing of the surf is louder here below, the night remains impenetrable for all but a few feet ahead.

Ding dong bell

Soon I am standing at the very spot where they say she fell. For the edge here is treacherous and the drop, while not particularly high, takes you directly into the waves below. The sea, seething back and forth in its constant struggle against the land.

Annabelle. Did you in sooth slip and fall that night? I stand on the edge, lamp thrust aloft, a human lighthouse, thinking perhaps I can shine a guiding light to bring my Annabelle home. For she remains in the ocean's cold embrace, she never returned to me. The sea does not easily give up its captives. I hold the lantern aloft and call her name, my voice echoing across the emptiness before me. Three times I call and the answer comes, the toll from beyond...

Ding dong bell

At once I am seized by a mad thought. A vision of my beautiful wife, bedraggled, ensnared, pulling the bell rope with all her might, calling me. The tolls are a cry for help! I dash instantly back along the path, ignoring the light rain that now falls and stings my eyes. I descend the slope and within minutes am crunching along the narrow shingle strand, the swaying lantern casting fantastic shadows as I go. Gasping in my zeal, I find a skiff and, with strength born of desperation, slide it down the shale and into the water. I'm coming Annabelle!

I know you wed me to ease your father's debts and I confess I wasn't a good husband, being something of an inebriate. But I was always sorry when I hit you, I always cared for you. And I am coming now, my darling, hastening to deliver you from your watery tomb, to pluck you from the jaws of death.

Ding dong bell

I follow the boat into the water, it runs cold around my knees. Setting the lantern down, I clamber in and begin pulling on the oars, back muscles cracking, unused to the strain and exertion. Ahead and to my right the bells sound again. Feverishly I work, my progress interminably slow, as though I remain fixed on the spot. Yet soon the pale shore has vanished from sight and I am alone on the dark glass. I bob in the gentle swell, the creak of oars and my own laboured breathing the only sounds to break the silence. Then there, again, closer now!

Ding dong bell

I pull the boat around and head directly for the sound. The rain is heavier now, streaming down my face in rivulets. I am oblivious to wet and cold, my only thoughts are of Annabelle. I stop again, straining my ears. The toll comes, rising from the depths directly beneath me. I am immersed in its rich, resounding tone as it rushes up like a vast air bubble, to burst in the air around me. I cast down the oars and pick up the lantern, leaning over the side of the boat to look down. The darkness swells beneath me, the lamp reflecting moon-like in the brine.

Then, there is something else. A movement, a pale glow, far below. Rising up, a pallid oval, blurred and indistinct. I cry out her name and wave the lantern, almost dropping it in my fervour. Nearer now, a shape taking form, a figure ascending from the plutonian depths. What phantasm is this? No! No phantasm, no construction of my febrile brain... it is Annabelle!

Full fathom five she lay but now has returned to me, her face upturned just below the surface. Her beauty has not faded but has suffered change. Her eyes are like pearls, her complexion blanched, her hair sinuous and green. She emerges, reaching for me with emaciated hands. I lean towards her and we embrace. I welcome the clasp of her bony arms, I press my lips to where hers used to be. My darling, my Annabelle.

As the bell tolls for one last time, she draws me slowly beneath the waves.

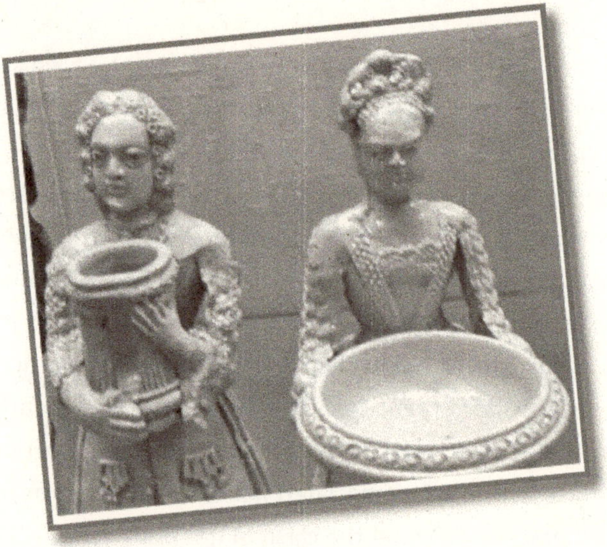

FEAR AT THE FITZ

"Then there was that queer business with Billings." Lethbridge lit a cigarette and drew on it, as he drew us in at the prospect of another story.

Chalmers ventured, "It's not another tale involving spiders is it? That gruesome anecdote of yours over lunch left me slightly queasy!"

Lethbridge chuckled and indicated the nearby display case with a wave of his hand. "No spiders, I promise! In actual fact it centres on these two characters."

We gathered around the case in question. It was by pure chance that the four of us, old school chums, all happened to be here in Cambridge, so we had taken the opportunity to share a hearty lunch at The Royal. Over coffee, Lethbridge had offered to show us round the Fitzwilliam Museum, his current stomping ground. Chalmers and I jumped at the chance, both being keen amateur historians. Phillips, ever the rational scientist, was less keen, knowing Lethbridge's penchant for the outré; yet up until now the tour had been most illuminating but entirely mundane. Trust Lethers to lull us into a false sense of security, saving the strangest until last!

Chalmers and I exchanged a brief grin as Phillips rolled his eyes at the prospect of another of Lethbridge's *weird tales*. Nonetheless we peered in at the objects indicated by our friend and guide.

"These two characters." He tapped on the glass, the middle shelf up. Amongst a display of tankards and dishes stood two figures; one male, one female, carved in some off white material. They looked like servants to me, dressed in old-fashioned clothing. The man carried a huge tankard, the woman held a large bowl in her arms. Tankard and bowl were being held forward, as though proffered to the viewer. Each figure was about eight inches high.

Chalmers, more the collector than I, rubbed his chin.

"Hmm, looks like Restoration period to me. Fairly crude workmanship, not particularly decorative, nor functional, as far as I can see."

Lethers nodded, "Spot on, old chap. Nothing that remarkable about them, you would think. Slightly odd features, you might say but that could be put down to poor workmanship. They've been dated to mid 17th century."

His features hardened. "But the effect seeing those figures had on Billings... and what he told me after... well ...."

Phillips broke the silence. "Billings, tall, willowy chap, pleasant type? Weren't you and he in the same outfit?"

"Yes," replied our guide. " C Company, 1st Cambridgeshire. We were at Passchendaele together."

Lethers stiffened slightly at the memory; God knows we all carried our memories of that awful time, even now, some fifteen years distant. He continued. "That's what made his reaction here all the more strange, for I know him to be a brave man. Yet at the sight of those apparently innocuous figurines, that brave man fell to a quivering heap, right here on this very spot."

"What on Earth could have caused that?" I asked.

Our old friend drew on his cigarette before replying. "That is a very good question, Jeffers. A very good question indeed. Tell you what, as our tour here has finished, let's retire to the Director's office. Sir Sydney has given me the key while he's away and I happen to know he has a fine single malt tucked away in his desk. I'll tell you the full story there."

So it was that we were soon ensconced in the said office, warming by the fire, tumblers in hand as Lethers took up the tale.

"I'd not seen Billings for a couple of years then happened to bump into him last August in Covent Garden, of all places. I was down in London on business at the time, engaged in an investigation. He told me he was on summer break from the courts, so I invited him up to Cambridge for a few days. Here, much as we have today, we caught up on old times and I showed him round the Fitz. That's when the incident occurred. And when I say quivering heap, that's exactly what I mean. Not since the trenches have I seen a man in such a funk. After, I brought him down to this very room, calmed him down and asked him what was wrong. He downed a slug of scotch - I really must get a replacement bottle before Sir Sydney returns - and then told me the following."

▲

I'm terribly sorry, Lethbridge. You must think me a real

chump acting like that. It's just the sight of those figurines... Well, why don't I tell you the whole thing from the start?

It was just over a year ago, June to be exact. I'd recently left my post at the Home Office and had a couple of weeks before taking up my new post at the law firm. I was born in the north, Mother was from Yorkshire, you know, so I decided on a little excursion, get out of the heaving metropolis for a while. I took the train up to York, spent a couple of days poking about the Minster, then began my tour.

Anyway, by my third day I was at Whitby. I had arrived late in the afternoon, only to find the local hotels were full, thanks to a literary festival taking place in the town. With nothing else to do, I wheeled my way down the West Cliff, via the amusingly named Khyber Pass, heading for the promenade, from where I planned to stroll on the beach and ponder my next move. From my elevated position, I could see that the strand was strangely empty, given the fact it was the first Saturday in June and the weather was glorious. On reaching the bottom of road, I espied a small crowd gathered along the promenade. Leaning my cycle against a rail, I edged through to find out what was occurring, which turned out to be a line of local constabulary walking slowly along the beach, eyes cast down. Closer by stood a senior looking type, presumably the officer in charge, overseeing the whole affair. Curious, I enquired of my neighbour, an elderly chap in overcoat and cap, what was happening.

"Thar's searching for a child," he replied. "Young lad went missing, thar's think he might have bin swept out to sea."

"How awful," I responded. One can only imagine the sheer hell the parents must go through in such a situation. "Was the lad local?" I asked.

"Nay," my new friend replied. "Lad was from Robin Hood Bay down coast. But if the bairn went in there, tide could carry him for miles."

Robin Hood Bay! Of course! I'd visited there as a child with Mother. We had visited a cousin of hers for a week once, I remembered, I must have been about six at the time.

Sun-tinged memories of a walk along the cliffs to the Bay sprang to mind, along with recollections of a large house and kindly man. Uncle Hugh, that was the chap! But the exact location of the house was beyond me.

Feeling a slight twinge of guilt that such a tragic event may have supplied a solution to my problem, I withdrew to a local public house, the landlord there kindly allowing me use his telephone. A quick call to Mother, currently taking the waters in Bath, furnished me with the address of her cousin; Hugh Balcombe, Stoupe House, south of Robin Hood Bay, just off the Ravenscar Road. Suitably fortified with information and a brandy, I set off.

It was a six or seven mile ride in pleasant conditions, though some of the hills were challenging. I wheeled through Robin Hood Bay and shortly after past the splendidly named Boggle Hole. By now, I was following a cliff top path, cut with steps in places. To my left the grey, majestic North Sea; to my right the glorious green fields of North Yorkshire. The path twisted and turned, but eventually I found a fork that took me back up onto the main road.

After stopping for directions from a resting field hand, I set off on the last stage of the ride. It was then that disaster struck. I admit, taken as I was with my surroundings, I had let my focus slip somewhat and may have been drifting towards the centre of the road. But the idiot in the car had no excuse, speeding as he was. Before I knew it, he was roaring up behind me and I was forced to swerve. My evasive manoeuvre saved me from immediate harm but caused me to hurtle into a ditch, taking a headlong dive over my handlebars, ending up in the hedge.

I jumped to my feet, waving a fist at the lone figure in the departing automobile, a two seater that roared up the hill ahead.

Shaken and somewhat scratched, I resumed my ride and was rewarded when, about fifteen minutes later, I found the side track that led to Stoupe House. I free-wheeled down the slope, now heading back towards the cliffs and sea. Halfway along stood the house, much as I remembered it from my childhood. What is referred to these days as a "Georgian pile", I believe. Two large bay fronts flanking a large, porticoed front door. Slipping off the bike, I wheeled it up the short gravelled drive and, using the heavy knocker, rapped thrice upon the glossy, bottle green door.

A wrinkled face appeared, regarding me with some alarm. I stammered a self-conscious introduction, suddenly aware that I had half a ton of local flora in my hair and was no doubt bleeding profusely from numerous small scratches. To his credit, and my relief, the manservant took me at my word and bade me enter the foyer. Leaning the bike against the wall, I followed him in and waited, eyeing the somewhat lurid artwork in the spacious hall. Seconds later, a slim figure, dressed in a maroon smoking jacket and open necked shirt, swept into view.

"George? Is that you? My word, you look awful!"

I laughed. "Yes, Uncle Hugh, it is. Apologies for my appearance. Took a bit of tumble off the old bike, I'm afraid."

Uncle Hugh warmly shook my hand and led me through to the sitting room. Minutes later, we were chatting over a cup of strong tea. Uncle asked after Mother and seemed pleased to hear she was in good health. The years had certainly been kind to him, he was much as I had remembered, being a touch over six feet tall, leonine grey hair swept back from strong, tanned face. He must be approaching seventy, I thought, yet appeared as full of vigour as a man half that age. Pleasantries over, he asked me the purpose of my visit. I explained my predicament, asking nothing more than a roof for the night. I thought I detected the briefest flicker of emotion flash across his face before the smile returned.

"Of course! Though I must admit you have rather caught me on the hop. We are preparing for a gathering tonight, I have friends visiting for dinner."

"Oh!" My face must have fallen. "Well, of course, if it is inconvenient I'm sure I can find somewhere in Ravenscar?"

"No, no, dear boy, I wouldn't hear of it! I'll get Stott to make up the attic room. Now, if you'll excuse me, I have some preparations to attend to for our soiree. Stott will carry your luggage up for you. Freshen up, then come down and join us in the dining room when you are ready."

That settled, I followed the aged Stott up to a small room set in the eaves, presumably an old servant's quarters judging from its size and location. It was pleasant enough however, a little cramped but with a marvellous view out over the rolling countryside that lay before the house. If I peered over to the right I could just make out the cliff tops and saw, with pleasure, the narrow ribbon of a path; presumably that same one I had walked along as a child to get to the golden beach beyond. Isn't it strange how our childhood memories are so often filled sunshine and laughter? What I wouldn't give now to magically erase the darker memories of later times and places.

But I digress. It was while admiring the view that the roar of a car engine became apparent and a two seat sportster hurtled into the front drive, squealing to a halt in a spray of gravel. It was the same car that had almost done for me earlier! I noticed there was now a passenger on board as well as a driver. I was quite intent on dashing downstairs to give the idiot a piece of my mind, when driver and passenger alighted, the former removing cap and goggles to reveal a rather attractive young lady. She tossed her short, auburn hair, throwing goggles, cap and gloves back into the car. Her passenger, a slim man of similar age, mid-twenties I judged, took out and lit a cigarette. I could just make out his voice, floating up to my lofty perch.

"Steady on, Pru, you'll bloody well get us killed one day, driving like that!"

The young lady responded with a pout, then a peck on the young man's cheek.

"What's wrong, Simon? Can't take the pace of the fast set?"

They both turned and moved out of sight below me, presumably as Stott opened the front door. Maybe it was the position I had twisted myself into, neck craned, maybe it was my earlier accident, maybe it was having been out in the sun all day. In any event, I came over a little faint and had to sit on the bed for a second. Having gathered myself, I decided a soak in the bath would cure all ills. There were some towels on the bed and Stott had pointed out the bathroom on the way up. As I stood again, I happened to see three more cars drawing up in front of the house, my Uncle's guests, I presumed. Still, I ran and enjoyed a hot bath, spending rather longer in there than I planned, the warm water soothing me into a nap.

By the time I had dressed for dinner and returned downstairs, the party were just arranging themselves around the dining table. I took up position as indicated by Stott and glanced around. Eleven guests, one of whom I recognised as the senior policeman I had seen at Whitby earlier that day. I noticed, curiously, that the seat at the head of table remained unoccupied, my Uncle being seated to its left. There was a low hum of conversation, one or two of the guests eyeing me with what I thought looked like hostility. The conversation was broken by Uncle Hugh tapping on his wine glass with a fork.

"Thank you all for coming on this special evening. I hope the night ahead proves illuminating to you all. You will have noticed we have an extra guest –"

"And one missing!" grumbled the elderly man to my right, eyeing the vacant chair.

"Fret not, Arthur, he is on the way and will be here presently." Uncle answered calmly. "As you will have noticed, we have an extra guest in our midst. Everyone, this is my cousin Mary's lad, George."

I nodded politely as Uncle went round the table with the introductions.

"Superintendent Nicholson." This was the passive faced policeman. "Major Ward-Jackson." A thick-set military type, complete with bristling moustache and ruddy complexion.

"Roger and Veronica Smedley." A middle-age, rather prim looking couple, she pinch faced, he with the expression of one long given over to a life of quiet acquiescence. Each so far either nodded or, in the case of the Smedleys, ignored me. Uncle continued round the table.

"Simon Mortimer." This to the fashionably attired car passenger, who guffawed slightly and raised his glass in toast.

"Miss Prunella Singleton." The car driver, who tilted her head coquettishly at me. She was also dressed in the latest style, complete with pearl necklace. Then, to the other side of the table.

"Professor Garstang." A rather odd looking individual, squat and shabbily dressed in rough tweeds. A typical academic, perhaps?

"Arthur Hargreaves." The elderly man who had spoken before. Well dressed, slightly stooped, with an air of concern and worry about him, as evidenced by the furrowed lines across his forehead. I muttered a greeting in response to each, my Uncle's introductions to the remaining guests being then interrupted by a hammering at the front door.

"Ah, here he is!" Uncle Hugh beamed. A figure strode imperiously into the room, Uncle announcing, "Ladies and gentlemen, this is Oswald Stansfield Jones."

The newcomer certainly cut a dash. Dressed in an expensive Savile Row double breasted suit, red open necked shirt and cravat. He peeled off his grey silk gloves, passing them and an ivory handled Malacca stick to the hovering Stott. The company stood, I followed suit, somewhat unaware of the protocol in these situations. Jones waved a hand, taking the seat at the head of the table. He had distinguished features, almost Roman one might say. His silver hair was cropped short, his countenance rather stern; I discerned something of a cruel twist about the thin lips. He glanced around the table, then his gaze fell fully onto me. I have to admit I have never felt so entranced by a gaze before or since. Bright blue, his eyes, dazzling like the sun off of the sea. I felt quite transfixed in that moment, pinned like a butterfly to a board. Then I was free as he turned and whispered to Uncle, who whispered in return. Seemingly satisfied, Jones nodded and placed both hands on the table. In a cut-glass accent, he spoke.

"Welcome, one and all to our little gathering. Some of you I know from prior occasions, for others, this is our first meeting. Nonetheless, I am sure that you are all aware of our purpose here this evening. For when the stars are right, our work may be done. But that lies a little ahead. Before then, as that other book says, let us eat, drink and be merry!"

There was a polite ripple of laughter as Stott and a maid began serving the first course. The meal was most pleasant, complimented with a selection of fine wines. Conversation was mixed around the table, some being quite voluble, others, such as my immediate neighbour Hargreaves, being rather withdrawn. I turned to Professor Garstang instead and enquired as to his work. He gave a broad smile and told me of how his research group had bought the old Coastguard Station out at the village ramparts. They were equipping it with tanks for the keeping of live marine animals in order to further research.

My Uncle leant forward to add, "It's a most interesting place, George. When the weather is bad and the sea rough, it's like being in a lighthouse. The big waves thunder on the outer wall making the whole building tremble, the spray swishes up over the windows and splashes on the roof before rushing down again. At high tide, in such weather, it isn't safe to leave the laboratory, lest the sea claim you for its own!"

The Professor was nodding in agreement, his eyes wide at the thought. That brought to mind an earlier incident, prompting me to voice a question. "Superintendent, did you find that missing boy at all?"

The policeman shook his head slowly. "I'm afraid not. When the sea takes someone, well... it is rare that the ocean gives up its catch."

He seemed disinclined to talk on the matter further. Quite understandable, I thought. Dealing with such unpleasantness is not conducive to jollity or light-hearted banter over the dinner table. Miss Singleton, seeking perhaps to lighten the mood, leaned forward and asked me what my own line of work was. I replied that I was in law and how it was dreadfully stuffy most of the time, but it did, at least give one a set of references; a framework, perhaps, a moral code by which to deal with one's fellow man. I saw Jones raise an eyebrow at this and, feeling somewhat emboldened after my third glass of wine dared to ask, "You disagree, sir?"

Jones frowned for a moment then gave a thin smile. "Do what thou wilt, that is the whole of the law."

I noticed a number of the company, the Smedleys in particular, gazing upon Jones with a look of complete admiration. Almost fawning, one might say. Like the Light Brigade, I decided to press on, regardless of numbers.

"But surely that is a recipe for anarchy? You can't have

everyone doing as they jolly well please. Society would fall apart, wouldn't it?"

"And what is society but a collection of fences put in place to pen in the sheep?" asked Jones. "The true man understands his destiny. Understands there are forces beyond the mundane. Understands how he may harness the powers of those forces in order to further his own purposes."

I was getting a bit lost now. "And what would those purposes be?"

Jones steepled his fingers and fixed me with his icy stare. "Why, whatever your will desires. To fully exercise your true will, to bend others to it, that is the law."

"I don't follow. What are we talking here, some kind of hypnotism? Mesmerism? Magic?"

It was the Professor who answered. "What is magic but science that we don't yet understand? So much lies beyond our comprehension. Why, there are things living in the sea that -

"Professor!" my Uncle interrupted. "I'm sure George doesn't want to hear about your experiments with jellyfish and the like. Now then, what say we have some dessert?"

The prospect of syllabub stilled the conversation but I was like a terrier tugging on a rope now. As the dessert things were cleared away, I piped up once more.

"You earlier mentioned something about the stars? Is that why you are gathered here tonight?"

I noticed an expression of concern flit across Uncle's face and he made to say something but Jones placed a hand on his forearm and spoke.

"Yes, you might say that, young man. Our little group here has a strong interest in the heavens and charting the procession of the stars. It is fascinating to consider the effects the position of the stars may have on our own planet, don't you think?"

I couldn't help it. I was a bit squiffy by now and the snort burst out before I could stop myself. "Astrology? Goodness me, isn't that a load of old hokum?"

I knew at once that I had gone too far. Whatever these peoples' beliefs, it was not my place to question them, least of all when I was a guest in someone else's home and least of all over the dinner table. Jones leant and whispered to Uncle once more, who stood and addressed the gathering.

"Well, ladies and gentlemen, I suggest we retire to the lounge for coffee or brandy. George, you are looking rather tired, might I suggest a nightcap before you turn in?"

Somewhat embarrassed, I stammered in agreement. A few minutes later, with the company now sat or stood around the lounge, I accepted a drink from Stott and, downing it in one, said my goodnights before retiring to my lofty chamber.

I was obviously more tired than I thought. I had barely reached my room and removed my outer clothing when I sank into the softness of the bed, falling instantly into the arms of Hypnos.

It was in that deep slumber that I had the most peculiar dream. I dreamt of a sound, a thin fluting melody that floated to my ears. I felt obliged to follow it, like a whip of gossamer thread. There was no doubt in my mind that this piping was a call, a summons, a summons to which I responded. In my dream I trod slowly down the narrow stairs, along the upstairs landing and finally down the main staircase into the hall. The night was bright, the whole house suffused with the soft radiance of a full moon, filtered through the net curtains. My sensation was not so much of walking as floating through the air, small eddies and currents gently pulling me onward.

The piping was louder in the hall, but still gentle and sinuous. I traced its source to the library. In my dream-state I felt myself drift across the thick carpet. The walls were lined with bookcases, the sound originating, impossibly, from behind one of them. No, not impossibly. My dream self found a small gap, an opening, the classic secret doorway so beloved of Gothic authors. Yet here it was. Placing my fingers in the dark crevice, with the lightest of pulls, the whole bookcase swivelled soundlessly, revealing a passage and steps beyond. Even in my dream state this did not same strange. Was not this whole stretch of coast steeped in tales of smugglers and secret ways?

I floated on, into the tunnel and down the thin steps, the music now echoing through the roughly hewn passageway. On and on it drew me, through twisting tunnels and further steps, down, down, until another sound, a deeper sound, underpinned that fluttering melody. A voice, low and monotonous. Not musical, but a chant. No words were audible but the bass tone rang vibrant through the narrow passage, increasing the urgency of my progress.

Closer, louder, the words now audible but words that made no sense. More sounds than words, guttural, polysyllabic, harsh. They brought a sense of dread with them, a hint of something alien, something beyond all forms of human thought and expression. As a dream within a dream, my mind was filled with vast undersea vistas of terrifying depth and beauty. A hint of cyclopean architecture brooding in unreachable green fathoms. And within that vision came another sound, a distant throb or pulse. I felt it signalled the first flickering of something stirring or awakening, of a looming presence turning its attention towards the surface.

Within the dream I could now detect a faint draught of cool air on my face and the fresh tang of the ocean in my nostrils. Rounding one last curve I saw ahead, lit in the ruddy glow of flaming torches, the interior of a cave, set close to the sea judging from the sound of hissing surf from outside its entrance. Around the cave, eleven figures gyrated and contorted, in various stages of dishabille. One blew on a bone flute, some writhed singly on the ground, others intertwined in unrestrained abandonment. It was a scene from Rowlandson, Bacchanalian revelry at its most depraved. And there, at its centre stood Stansfield Jones. clad in dark robes, hood cast back to reveal his upturned face, arms raised in supplication as he continued that unearthly chant.

I stood transfixed in the shadows as the chant reached its peak, the group squirming in paroxysms of lust, now gathering to kneel around Jones, arms aloft in adjuration. With a final cry, the group shuddered as one and fell prone to the sandy floor. Jones was still as a statue, face strained, the sinews in his neck standing out like wires. His lips writhed wordlessly, his fingers curled and grasped the cool air. There it was again, that distant pulse.

"The Sleeper stirs!" Jones cried. "Let the Servers bring forth the sacrament!"

He span towards the cave entrance, from where another sound could be heard. The slapping of bare feet on wet sand, presaging an scene that will remain engraved on my brain until my last expiration.

Two additional figures now entered my dream. At first, they

were no more than vague outlines of darkness against the softer light of the night sky. Slowly they shuffled forward into the cavern, features becoming more distinct. One was male, one was female. Both were dressed in archaic costume, clothing that dated back centuries. Each held a container, the male a large pot, the female a bowl. Now they came full into view, their features... any doubts about this being a nightmare were dispelled at that moment. For the features of those things were barely human.

Squat faces, bulging eyes widely spaced, such features could only live in nightmare, surely? Jones smiled and moved back, the rest of the group gathering around the newcomers. Unblinking, discoloured tongues occasionally flicking over their flabby lips, the pair lifted their vessels, proclaiming in unison with croaky voices,

"Behold the sacrament! Partake, those of you would glorify the Father! Partake, those who would share in the glory of days to come! Partake, ye who worship Dagon, ye who would seek to wake the Star Spawn below!"

The vessels were now lowered and dipped towards the congregation, who reached in and feasted thereof. That is when the nightmare deepened once more, for in that infernal light I caught a glimpse of what those vessels contained. Parts. Parts! Parts of a child, God help me, swimming in a dark liquid. Parts that were held up by that hellish group before being greedily consumed.

I saw them all, Uncle Hugh, the Smedleys, the Professor, all of them, dark juices running down their chins and chests as they revelled in the unthinkable. Then that pulse again, followed by such a rumbling and quaking that the whole cavern trembled. In the dream, I stumbled, fell headlong into darkness and knew no more.

I awoke, in my attic chamber, to blessed sunlight and birdsong. Shaking myself clear of the webs of sleep I moved to the window, opening it wide and taking in a breath of fresh Yorkshire air. I noticed I was wearing a nightshirt, though had no memory of getting changed last night. In fact, my memory was somewhat hazy all round. It was only as I sat that I began to recall that terrible dream. So vivid was it, that I was prompted to note it down in my journal. An odd thing, you might think, but a journal is there to record all experiences, pleasant or not.

Dressed and washed, I repaired downstairs, summoned by the smell of breakfast. There is little more to tell of my visit. Uncle Hugh was in place, clad in dressing gown, looking a little dishevelled. As he motioned for me to join him, Stott appearing with a plate of kippers, he asked if I had slept well.

"I did indeed, Uncle," I replied, nudging the kippers around the plate with my fork. For some reason I had very little appetite this morning.

"Well, you were a little worse for wear last night! A touch too much wine, perhaps, coupled with that knock you had!"

I smiled in agreement, I'm sure Uncle was right. It had been an eventful day and I had drunk rather more than usual; the slight throbbing in my temples attested to that. I enquired as to how the rest of the evening went.

"Very well," said Uncle. "You missed nothing except some chat, then we went outside to do a little star gazing. I do hope we did not disturb you?"

I shook my head, gratefully accepting the pot of tea that Stott carried in.

"Excellent!" Uncle dabbed his lips with a napkin and stood. "Well, I have a few things to attend to today, but you stay as long as you like. Let Stott know when you're ready to leave and I'll come and see you off." With that, he was gone.

Pushing the plate aside, I finished my tea and rubbed my eyes, which eased the dull ache somewhat. Then a thought struck me. Checking to see that Stott was not around, I moved swiftly across the hall into the library. All stood as it had in my dream, three of the walls filled with large bookcases. In vain, I searched along them for some switch or mechanism. The cases remained resolutely still despite my prodding and poking, with no sign of an opening. I was startled by a cough behind me. Stott stood in the doorway.

"Will that be all, sir?"

I mumbled something about "just browsing the books" and returned to my room. Fifteen minutes later I was back downstairs, ready to go. Stott had brought the bike round to the front and Uncle shook my hand on the front step.

"Do give my regards to your mother. And take care, George. Do take care."

With that I set off back towards Whitby and never saw Uncle Hugh again. By the next week I was back in London at my new post, thrown into the world of criminal law. It was hard for me to adjust but I eventually settled in and have been doing well at the firm ever since. Any thoughts of my nightmare that evening faded over time; I suppose I put it down to wine and the accident. Nonetheless, I have found myself, on the odd occasion, waking with a hoarse cry in the middle of the night.

Not that that is unusual in men who have been through our experiences.

No, it was the sight of those figurines that threw me into such a blind funk. Those damned figurines! For I tell you, they are the exact replica of those terrible servants I saw in my dream. The exact replica, down to the last detail! How can I explain that, except to say they must have been sculpted from life? Yet those figurines date back centuries, no one can live that long, can they? Worst of all, if those figurines are real people, then it must be reasoned that my dream was real too. It wasn't a dream at all, Lethbridge... it actually happened!

▲

Lethbridge let out a sigh and refilled his tumbler. Phillips spoke first.

"Obvious, isn't it? Chap had a bang on the head, drank too much vino, had a bad dream. Later on he sees these figurines that look something like those in his nightmare, there we go, two plus two equals five."

Lethbridge just smiled in response. Chalmers spoke up next.

"Got to say, old chap, Phillips has hit it on the head there. Surely you can't imagine any of this was real, Lethers? Human sacrifice? Sea monsters and magicians? In Yorkshire?"

Lethbridge looked to me and raised his eyebrows, knowing how up I was on various snippets of lore from around the British Isles.

"It's not *that* unheard of," I admitted, quickly adding at seeing Phillips' expression, "though all strictly myth and legend, of course. There's the Hob, a fish-man type creature seen at Runswick Bay. Then there's the pair of mermaids reportedly caught at Stathes, they eventually escaped from the nets. Both are on the same stretch of coast. Then you have Whitby itself." I leaned forward, warming to my topic. "There was the legend of old Maggie, the witch. They say on the day she died a huge storm came in and put part of the town under water. I believe you can still see the hag stones displayed on some doorways up there, to ward off evil. "

Phillips groaned and shook his head. Lethbridge smiled again and gestured with his cigarette.

"There's more," he stated. "Fairfax's *Deamonologia* of 1621 details witchcraft cases throughout the area. There are also various examples in the York Assizes of witchcraft trials."

"Poor lonely, old women who owned a cat, no doubt," scoffed Phillips.

"Not always women." Lethers, as always, left his strongest cards until last. "In 1724, a certain Mathew Boumer of Newcastle was accused of witchcraft and *trafficking with powers from the sea*. He was sentenced to be hanged by one Lord Erskine, and his property and goods confiscated by the Crown. Some of those possessions were later donated to us here at the Fitz. Can you guess what they might include?"

"The figurines?" grinned Chalmers.

Lethers returned the grin. "Yes, the figurines. And, while my research has not been conclusive, it seems there may be a direct family line connecting this Boumer and our Billing's Mr Jones.

"Circumstantial!" announced Phillips, crossing his arms. "Coincidence!"

"There was a book also, part of Boumer's estate. Some form of grimoire, I believe, entitled *Cthäat Aquadingen*. The

Fitz handed it over to the University Library, it's now part of the Manby Collection."

"Some sort of spell book, is it?" I asked.

"I believe so, or full of rituals, at least. I've had only the briefest glimpse, what with all the books being transferred over to the new building. From my short inspection, it primarily details rituals concerning some ancient, aquatic god."

"Dagon," Chelmers said. "Billings said those *servants* mentioned Dagon. Fish god, wasn't he? Philistines, if I 'm not mistaken?"

"You're not," Lethers replied. "But that appears to be but one branch of a much older cult. One, we can gather, that is still in operation. I shall be investigating that matter further once my duties at the Fitz are completed."

"So now we have magic books to add into the stew!" responded Phillips. "Are there any concrete facts at all in this yarn?"

Lethbridge continued. "Well, there is the question of the tremor. It is beyond any doubt that on the 7th June last year, at around one-thirty in the morning, the north-east coast of England was hit by an earthquake. The largest ever recorded in these Isles, in fact!"

"Coincidence again!" pleaded Phillips but Lethers was well into his stride by now.

"That inspired me to carry out more research. The earthquake was centred on Dogger Bank, way out to sea. Billings spoke of the feeling of something "stirring" or "awakening". Perhaps this ritual was designed to summon whatever it is that slumbers at Dogger Bank?"

"Bit of a reach, isn't it, old chap?" asked Chalmers.

"Perhaps. But consider this! If you go back over the records, you will find there has been a similar earthquake every ninety years or so. 1931, 1839, 1748, 1659. Even further back, there are local reports of such quakes."

Lethers paused to fix us with his stare. "Now, of course, in days of old they could not determine the epicentre or measure the strength of an earthquake; but they do seem to be getting stronger. What's more, these earthquakes correspond with certain astronomical alignments. I had one of the chaps at the Observatory check it all over for me. He tells me the next such alignment is due in 2023. Perhaps a ritual then will lead to the strongest tremor yet; and that might mean that whatever lies out there in the deeps will be fully woken and rise up. It would be interesting to see what it is, don't you think?"

INNSMOUTH ECHOES

RETURN TO PROVIDENCE

The lights of my ancestral home
Shine dimly through the snow
The gates creak open at my touch
The wind moans soft and low

For many years I've wandered far
And studied ancient lore
The books that tell of hidden things
And those who came before

Return to Providence
Back to the ties that bind
Return to Providence
Who knows what I shall find

I've seen what dwells beyond the veil
Heard their whisperings and schemes
I know the faceless King in tattered robes
And that which is dead but dreams

Now summoned back by duty's call
I return to home and hearth
To claim that which is rightfully mine
And has been since my birth

Return to Providence
Back to the ties that bind
Return to Providence
Who knows what I shall find

For tonight in caverns far below
For the ritual we shall gather
I shall speak the words and receive the gift
From the thing that was my father

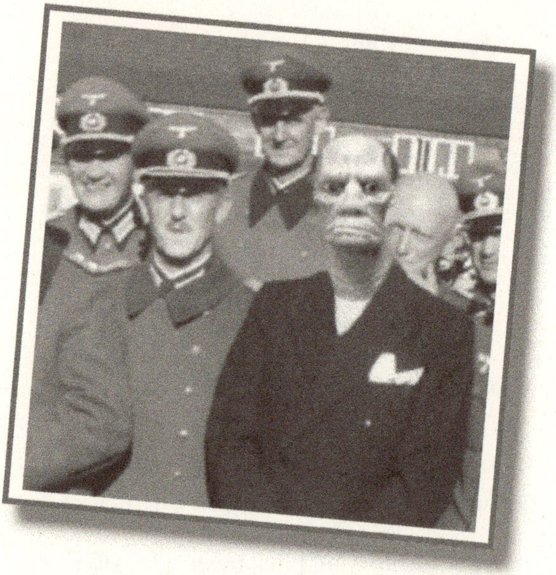

U-873

"Dive! Dive! Dive!" The alarm bell sounded and everyone rushed to their posts. We had been running at periscope depth, thanks to the new Schnorchel device but our wake, I guessed, had been spotted by an aircraft The Skipper squeezed past me, buttoning up his jacket.

"Report!" he barked.

"Taking us down to one hundred metres, sir," I replied.

"Good, Karl. Keep us on course. We can expect to see more of our American friends the closer we get to the coast. I'll be back in my quarters. Our passenger was about to reveal our secret orders when the alarm sounded."

"About time!" I grumbled and the Skipper smiled in response. Typical of Cool Hans as he was known. Fregattenkapitän Hans Steinhof, Knights Cross with Oak Leaves and Crossed Swords. Ten patrols, thirty ships sunk. And me? Wachoffizier Karl Seitz, Knight's Cross, eight patrols. I'd been second-in-command on many of those trips and never once seen the Skipper flustered. Not until this mission.

I cast my mind back to the dockside at La Pallice where the

new boat was being outfitted prior to our mission.

"Damn and blast it, Karl!" The Skipper had sworn at me. "As if it's not enough to have the SS aboard, they've foisted a mad scientist on us too!"

I raised my eyebrows and shrugged in sympathy. "We are to take them somewhere?" I'd enquired.

"I've not received the full orders yet," the Skipper had replied. "But my best guess is South America. Probably an escape mission for our Doctor. The rats have begun to desert the ship, it seems!"

It was not spoken but we both knew the truth; the Reich was finished. The big offensive in the Ardennes had failed, the Soviets were within striking distance of our Eastern borders. However, it was still dangerous to be overheard spreading "defeatist" talk, the Gestapo and SD still had ears everywhere, even on a U-boat.

Now, here we were half-way across the Atlantic and still we did not know our precise mission. Furthermore, our passengers made the crew uneasy. Well one was *Waffen SS*, Major Kruger. The uniform naturally put one on edge and the man's scarred features and twisted posture only added to the overall effect. Eastern Front, we assumed, but he was not the type you asked. He, at least, seemed human. Our other guest, the scientist, well... when you bumped into him in the dark confines of the U-boat, you really got the creeps.

Eisner, that was his name. Unblinking eyes stared at you through thick, rimless spectacles. He was short, heavy-set, bald with an ever present leer on his pudgy face. I overheard some of the crew refer to him as "Toadman". I had to caution them. Accurate as it may be, Eisner was *Ahnenerbe*. Even the regular

SS feared them, Himmler's personal research department. He had arrived with two small crates, nailed shut and unmarked. Fortunately he mostly stayed in his quarters leafing through some old book and chuckling strangely to himself.

"Screw sounds ahead, sir." called Drexler the hydrophone operator.

"Take us down to one five zero meters, half speed ahead." The crew acknowledge and snapped to their task. They were a good bunch, most of us had been together for two years now. The sound of screws was growing, alongside the ping of sonar. I nudged Strobel. "Leo, best fetch the Skipper."

By the time the Skipper was back, the screws were overhead. Two of them now, destroyers, from the sound of it. The Skipper took over, calmly issuing orders as the enemy vessels circled above. We all knew what came next. Depth charges. Sure enough, the sonar pings stopped and every man there automatically braced himself. A breathless silence before the dull thumps, four in quick succession, the last one rocking the boat violently. I noticed that Kruger had joined us. To give him his due, the bastard looked as unperturbed as the Skipper.

"All stop, take us to the bottom," the Skipper ordered, then smiled at Kruger. "We have some friends upstairs, it seems they do not appreciate our presence in their waters. You might be more comfortable in your quarters, Herr Major."

Kruger gave a twisted grin in return. "I am perfectly comfortable here, Herr Kapitan. I was at Kursk, you know?"

The Skipper shrugged, turning his attention back to our predicament. Another brace of depth charges, one very close. The lights flickered as the boat rocked again. I called for damage reports from all sections. That was when Eisner made an appearance in the control room, squeezing his bulk through the door, his cheap grey suit dark with sweat marks under the arms. He moved straight to the Skipper.

"What is the meaning of this? Why have we stopped?"

"Perhaps you have not noticed, Herr Doktor, we are currently under attack from enemy forces."

"Then surely we should be moving, can we not outrun them?"

Even Kruger shook his head at this. Everyone else was suddenly very busy at their own tasks. The Skipper sighed and rubbed the bridge of his nose. The retort being framed on his lips was never delivered as the next brace of depth charges exploded. A little further away this time but still enough to rattle the hull. Eisner gave a curiously high-pitched squeal and scuttled back to his quarters.

As the sound of screws receded, the Skipper ordered us up off the floor and back on course at 100 metres. He motioned for me to follow, along with Kruger. The three of us crammed into the Skipper's quarters as he produced a bottle of Korn, pouring each of us a generous measure. Eisner appeared and hovered in the doorway.

"Anyway, as I was saying before we were so rudely interrupted..." Kruger removed a manila envelope from inside his tunic and handed it to the Skipper. He smoothly slit it open, slid out the single sheet of paper within, scanned it quickly, then passed it to me. It was blank apart from a set of co-ordinates, followed by a single sentence. "You are to follow directly the orders of Dr Eisner in all matters." The signature at the bottom read *H. Himmler*.

"It appears we are under your command, Herr Doktor," the Skipper said curtly. A crafty grin spread across Eisner's loathsome features.

"At last. Perhaps now we can focus on our mission. For it is of the utmost importance in securing our final victory!"

Even Kruger looked surprised at that. Assigned, he had told us, to be Eisner's bodyguard, I imagine he thought, as we did, that this was an escape mission to South America. Instead, the co-ordinates lay just off the North East coast of America.

"Is there nothing else you can tell me, Herr Doktor?" the Skipper asked.

"Only this. Through various avenues of research, my superior, Obersturmbahnnführer Reiss, has become aware of the existence of a most powerful weapon. One that presently lies hidden and dormant just off the coast of mainland USA. My mission is to make contact with the individuals who possess this weapon and persuade them to unleash its full fury on the decadent Americans. Believe me, gentlemen, we have the potential to unleash a power that will bring the Allies begging to the negotiating table. Then a new dawn will arise for the Reich!"

His eyes shone at this point and spittle gathered at the edges of his flabby lips. There was an awkward pause then Kruger gave a cough. "Well, that is welcome news indeed. I am sure we would all drink to final victory and the wisdom of the Fuhrer!"

Mechanically we all raised our glasses level to the third tunic button, in the approved fashion, and with a desultory "To the Fuhrer!" drained them. That seemed to end the meeting and I was briefly left with the Skipper before returning to my watch.

"I don't like this, Karl but what can we do? A direct order from the Reichsführer himself? If anything goes wrong, he'll have the family of every crew member rounded up by the Gestapo and shipped to one of his blasted camps."

"Could there be such a weapon?" I wondered.

The Skipper snorted. "Fairy stories. We lost this war two years ago. All that remains is to do our best by the crew, eh Karl? So let's follow orders for now and see what will be."

Just over a week later we found ourselves stealthily approaching America's Atlantic Coast. Many of the old sweats had been here before, in the happy time known as the *American Shooting Season.* That was back in '42, when the Amis had obviously thought themselves untouchable, sailing up and down their coast with lights ablaze and no escorts. They became quick learners, though it was a painful lesson; our next visit to this part of the world had not been so happy. In fact, we had barely escaped with our lives, thanks mainly to the abilities of our Cool Hans.

Our journey had been uninterrupted since the attack, the new boat was able to operate underwater for much longer periods of time. The crew even became accustomed to the presence of our odd-looking passenger. Sailors are an adaptable bunch, if prone to superstition. In fact, one or two even engaged Eisner in conversation, notably our bookish radio operator, Thomsen.

Spotting the book that Eisner often carried, Thomsen enquired after it. Our guest gave his curious, gurgling laugh before explaining.

"It is a rare work indeed, the *Cthäat Aquadingen*. Few copies remain, this one was obtained by our agents some years ago, taken from beneath the very noses of the English. Not that the fools realised what they had, it was locked away in one of their university libraries!" The rest of the crew had backed away a little but Thomsen's interest was piqued.

"It is a history book then, or tells of war?" he asked.

Eisner hugged the large tome to his chest. "History of a sort. It tells of those who came before and who will come again. It tells of how one might contact them and it tells of beings from the stars, who still live but are imprisoned deep in aquatic tombs. In fact, there is one such tomb close to England itself according to the book, but access would be uncertain and difficult in British waters. Instead, we must meet our American friends who claim they have dominion over something much more suited to our purposes!"

Over Eisner's shoulder I could see Strobel circling his finger around his temple, the rest of the crew looking away or stifling laughter. Eisner caught himself, perhaps feeling he had passed on too much information and scuttled back to his quarters.

That had been last night. Now, in daylight hours we lay silent and still on the ocean floor. Come nightfall we rose slowly through the dark waters to surface some five kilometres off the coast. The cool night air flowed soft and fresh through the hatch as we climbed into the conning tower. The lookouts, in their red-lensed goggles, took position fore and aft as our two passengers joined the Captain and I. The sea was calm, just a light swell and above us the Milky Way shone brilliant and pure. For a moment one could believe that the war was far distant. Eisner checked his watch and held aloft a gemstone. The Skipper caught my eye and raised his eyebrows. Nothing happened. We remained in place for another five minutes. Me, I was feeling increasingly anxious about being immobile and on the surface so close to enemy territory. Kruger was as impassive as ever, cupping a foul smelling Russian cigarette in his palm. The Skipper betrayed his agitation by tapping his foot. He was about to order us back down when the gem began to emit a soft glow. Eisner's face was fish-belly pale in its light and I noticed his lips moving slowly as if in prayer. The glow increased, a wan yellow light, I could see the Skipper growing more agitated. Then there was a soft whisper from the fore look-out, "A light, sir. There!"

We followed the man's outstretched hand to see a flickering greenish light landward. The dark smudge of the coast lay behind it, I assumed it must be coming from some kind of craft. My assumption was proven correct when the faint chug of an engine drifted across the waves, heralding the appearance of a rather shabby lobster boat, crewed by two indistinct figures. The boat heaved to, one of the figures clambering aboard. He made for the forward hatch, I called down for it to be opened. The figure disappeared into the interior, his own craft already casting off and heading back into the night. Eisner, gem returned to his jacket, was wearing a broad smile. "Shall we go below, gentlemen?" he suggested.

We dutifully obeyed, our craft sinking once more into the Atlantic depths. Back down in the control room there was some commotion, the men were clucking like hens. I grasped Strobel's arm and asked him what was going on. He pointed back along the boat.

"Our new passenger. He seems to have put the wind up the crew."

I was about to scoff when a figure shuffled in through the forward door. There was a collective gasp, even Cool Hans seemed taken aback. In the glow of the bulkhead the newcomer's skin looked distinctly pale green. He wore a baggy coat that concealed a hunched, queerly shaped frame. The head was also misshapen, hairless, the face oddly protruding forward. Large, milky eyes, unblinking, a snub nose and wide, thin-lipped mouth. As he shambled closer I caught the tang of his body odour too. Believe me, after a few weeks on a U-boat it takes a special kind of smell to cut through the everyday fug that develops; that unforgettable blend of sweat, damp, mould and diesel. But cut through it did as the figure moved past me, a flabby arm brushing me aside.

The man made no attempt to speak to anyone but shuffled directly for Eisner, who raised his hands in greeting. He looked like the cat that has the cream. The newcomer made a croaking sound in response and the two disappeared, Eisner summoning Kruger over his shoulder.

The odd pair remained in conference in the map room, Kruger on guard at the door, hand on pistol, for over two hours. The rest of us carried out our usual duties, napped or played cards or chess. The Skipper was eventually summoned to the room, then returned about ten minutes later and spoke over the announcement system.

"Men, I can now reveal that we are embarked on a mission of great importance. Shortly, we shall be establishing contact with a group of American dissidents who have access to a powerful weapon. If we are able to persuade these people to give us access to this weapon, I am reliably informed we can change the course of the war, even at this stage. I know every man here will do his duty for his colleagues and the Fatherland. Please stand by for further instructions and good luck."

Then he turned to me. "Prepare our dinghies, Karl, we are surfacing. Once on top, proceed ahead slow, bearing 40 degrees to port. I want a shore team ready, eight men, reliable ones."

I touched the peak of my cap and relayed the Skipper's orders. Soon we were again breathing the sweet night air, the boat softly cutting through the shallow waves towards the dark smudge of land. Our passengers were all present, the newcomer included. As we drew closer to the shore, that man whispered something to Eisner, who relayed it to the Skipper.

"He says be careful here, Herr Kapitan. There is a large reef directly ahead. Some parts are visible, others lay hidden beneath the waves."

Instructions were passed down the tube and, sure enough, the dark line of a reef could be seen jutting above the waters to our starboard side. I had the queerest notion that something moved as we drew close, sliding off the reef back into the sea. Some marine creature, no doubt, or a trick of the light. A minute or so later, the control room relayed reports of strange, banging noises along our hull. Eisner wheezed, shoulders jiggling. "Do not be concerned," he said. "Our new friends are merely curious."

The tappings passed and, at another suggestion from our American guest, the boat was brought to a halt. The pair of dinghies were readied and we took our places; myself, the Skipper, our three passengers and the eight shore crew, armed with an assortment of rifles, grenades and an MP-40. Instructions had been given to Strobel and the boat silently sank as we paddled away into the dark, with orders to lay at periscope depth until our return.

The swell felt much heavier in the dinghies but the crew were strong lads and, following directions, we drew into a harbour. Ahead, three figures waited atop a jetty, one holding aloft a bulls eye lantern which cast a finger of yellow light across the water. Moored, we climbed up the jetty, four of our men carrying Eisner's crates. Leaving one pair behind to safeguard our escape route, we followed the figures.

My memories of that meeting are somewhat overshadowed by subsequent events, so you will forgive me if I am less than comprehensive in my description of that place. I have an impression of decaying buildings, of an old harbour, of the strange, shuffling gait of our escorts. Above all, I recall the most distinctive odour, a particular taint in the fresh, sea air that one could almost taste. Viscous, fishy, rotten. At the end of the harbour stood a large warehouse, not in the best of condition but apparently still in use. We were led inside. I noticed our crew men not engaged in carrying the crates had their firearms prepared for action, the dismal surroundings doing nothing to dispel the nervousness which had infected the crew since the arrival of our newest passenger.

The stench inside was stronger and the floor of the place was littered with indeterminate debris. A large figure detached itself from the gloom as we approached. I noticed our guides faltered somewhat, making a small bowing movement as the figure drew close. It was dressed in a dark, hooded robe, somewhat akin to that of a monk, I thought, though a monk of no conventional denomination given the curious patterns that decorated the garment. From within the hood shone two baleful eyes. It was difficult to make out any other features, enshadowed as they were, the only light source being the single lantern of our guides. Even Eisner seemed nervous, the robed figure gave off a palpable sense of menace. One of our guides spoke, again that croaking voice. I do not speak English so had no notion of what was said. However, the next words were in stilted German, from the robed figure himself.

"Welcome, gentlemen. I thank ye for your visit. It has been made clear that ye have certain items that are of interest to us and, in return, ye seek knowledge of how we may smite thine enemies? Be this correct?"

Eisner, all smiles and jitters, confirmed that this was indeed so. I could not understand the man's obsequiousness; you would have thought we were meeting the Holy Father himself in the Vatican, not some American insurgent in a run-down coastal port. Nevertheless, the two began to speak, the Skipper and I exchanging glances and doing our best to stay alert and on guard to treachery. At a signal, the two crates were brought up and opened, revealing the contents within, much to the delight of our host. I caught only a vaguest glimpse of the items, some jewellery and an oddly-shaped idol of some kind, rather pagan and primitive from the looks of it. Eisner also handed over his beloved book, though it obviously pained him to do so. Kruger stood motionless off to one side, hand on holster, eyeing all with alert suspicion. The robed figure was speaking again, if you can call such a strange voice "speaking".

"Excellent. And now, for our part of the bargain. Let me

show ye our weapon. Though I might warn ye that the sight of it may be disturbing to your sensibilities." I thought I caught the hint of a dry chuckle and the Skipper bristled at the sound.

"Really? Let me inform you, sir, that I am an Officer of the Kreigsmarine, a veteran of many sea battles. We Germans do not rattle so easy!"

Eisner appeared aghast at this intrusion but, if the robed figure took umbrage, he gave no sign. He merely shuffled closer, that terrible odour growing stronger, to peer into the Skipper's face.

"A veteran of sea battles, ye say? I wonder how much ye really know about the sea? Shall I tell thee? Ye know nothing! Nothing, I say!" This last was delivered in a sharp bark that had the Skipper flinch and our boys instinctively tighten grips on their firearms. Eisner intervened, to pour oil on troubled waters.

"Now, now there is no cause for disagreement. It was just a figure of speech, I am sure. Yes, we would be delighted to see the weapon. We had heard that the government raid some years back had...neutralised it. I take it this is not the case?"

"It is not," hissed the robed one. "A minor inconvenience. That mere men could destroy what our Lord has delivered unto us is unthinkable. Let us move to the beach and I will show ye."

Beach was a generous word for the narrow strip of sand on which we found ourselves but nonetheless it was just pleasant enough to be outside in the air again, local stink or not. As we watched, the robed figure brought forth a wickedly curved dagger from the sleeve of his vestment, stepping forward until the cold surf was at his ankles.

In his croaking tone he began a chant in a language that I have not heard before or since. If language it was, for I could make out no words amongst the guttural syllables. As he chanted, the curious figure made certain gestures and motions with the dagger. At some unknown signal, one of our guides hurried forth, head bowed, to join the figure in the surf. He rolled back the sleeve of his coat, revealing a mottled and twisted limb, offering it to the robed one. As the chant increased in intensity, the dagger was slashed viciously across the man's arm, producing a steady flow of blood, black in the dim light, that dripped into the sea. The man retreated to shore as the chanting reached a peak. It finished with the robed one, arms aloft, screaming out to sea, "Ya! Ya! Ya!"

And then... nothing happened. Eisner seemed concerned, wringing his pudgy hands together. Kruger, eyes narrowed, stood impassive behind him. The locals were motionless, heads bowed. The Skipper and I exchanged another glance as the robed one retreated back onto the sand. Our men remained nervous, though were steadied by a quiet word from the Skipper. I was about to make a comment of my own when it happened.

It began as a small bubbling on the sea surface, about five metres out. The bubbling grew in intensity and there was a vague impression of some bulk coming to the surface. For a crazy moment, I imagined our boat had followed us in and was about to surface, impossible as that was. What eventually rose, dripping and obscene, out of the water was no less impossible. I cannot bear to think of it even now, how can such a thing exist in a sane world?. But then given the events of those terrible years, I wonder if the human race can make any claim to sanity at all?

Blurred impressions are all that remain, as though my

senses were unwilling or unable to take in all details of that unholy form. A vast bulk, not solid, like a whale, but flowing, writhing, changing. Like some vast gastropod but no, for even they have a definite form, pulpous and yielding as it may be. This thing truly had no shape! At one glance it looked entirely solid, at another flowing like mercury, at yet another flabby, or even non-corporeal. And the eyes.... boiling and heaving in the whole mass were a score of eyes, disappearing and reforming as that gelatinous bulk glistened and squirmed in the brine. There were mouths also, or what my struggling brain translated as mouths. The thing broke surface and spread like an oil slick, tendrils reaching out on all sides as those hellish apertures gaped and yawned hungrily.

The locals had all fallen to their knees. Eisner looked to be in the throes of sexual ecstasy. The Skipper was stunned into silent shock. Our men... bless them, our men... One of them, Tannert, I think, put three rounds of rapid fire into the thing, an instinctive reaction, perhaps, to such a blasphemous sight.

The shots broke the tableau. There was no discernible effect on the creature but the robed one turned and with a hiss slashed at Tannert with the dagger. Tannert took a slice to the arm before reeling back, bringing up his rifle in defence. The robed figure turned, avoiding the rifle butt and sank his dagger to the hilt in the chest of Tannert's companion The other locals sprang up, two of them falling as shots rang out from our rifles. The Skipper stepped in and punched the robed one squarely in the face, before drawing his pistol and shouting, "Back to the dinghies!"

The leader crashed back into his remaining followers, their tangling fall giving us just enough time to regain the harbour wall and race for the jetty. Eisner was babbling, clawing at us as we passed, as if to impede our progress. Kruger locked eyes with the Skipper, calmly drew his pistol and blasted the back of Eisner's head away. Now we were racing along the harbour, a croaking cry from behind us winging out into the night. The cry was answered as a score of shambling figures burst from the nearby street and buildings. We weren't going to make it!

The lads at the dinghies had heard the commotion and were laying down covering fire for us. But in the dark and with only two rifles, they were barely delaying our pursuers. We made the head of the jetty when Kruger turned at snatched the MP-40 from our crewman.

"You go ahead," he snarled, "I'll hold this inhuman rabble off!"

"Kruger!" shouted the Skipper, "It's suicide, man! Come on!"

But Kruger gave a grim smile. "I'm a physical wreck, Herr Kapitan, my time has come. The dream is over. Get your men away, save them and yourself."

With that he turned, pulled back the bolt with a click and lay burst after burst of automatic fire at the approaching horde. That did the trick, we virtually flew into the dinghies and began a furious paddle away from the shore. As we went out I turned back, to see Kruger throw the now empty sub-machine gun at the gathering throng. He drew the pistol and made several shots as they swarmed at him. The last bullet, he saved for himself.

"Kapitan!" cried Tannert, raising his rifle to fire into the sea. I thought he had gone mad but then saw, with alarm, dark figures in the water, moving like fish but man shaped! They were converging on us quickly, the rifle fire having little effect.

"You men, keep rowing!" cried the Skipper from the other dinghy. "Karl, keep your boat close to ours. Grenades! Who has grenades?"

Two of the men fumbled and produced grenades, unscrewing the caps and throwing them without delay towards those undulating figures. Spouts of water rose with a crump, our efforts rewards by the sight of a number of figures floating motionless on the surface. Our rowers redoubled their efforts and we were soon back at the rendezvous point.

I pointed back toward the shore. A light could be seen flickering angrily from some high point on land. We knew not its meaning, wishing only for the reappearance of our beautiful boat. Sure enough there came another bubbling, I wondered with a start if it might presage the appearance of that thing again. But now, first the bows, then the rest of the ship broke the surface and we clambered aboard before the hatches were even open.

"Close up!" ordered the Skipper, "Get us out of here, Strobel, but mind that damned reef!"

Meanwhile the medic had appeared to fuss around us. Two men were missing, fallen or snatched out of the dinghy, perhaps. One was babbling incoherently, tearing at his own face. He had to be sedated before being carried below. We were all in shock, I imagine but we were by no means clear yet. I joined the Skipper in the conning tower, the better to guide our pilot past that reef. Shiny and black it lay, but not bare as before. For now it swarmed with bodies. Mercifully, at this distance and in the dark, it was difficult to make out their full details. Man-sized, certainly, but with disturbing silhouettes and motions that were more marine than mammal. A wave of the things plunged off the reef towards us and we soon heard the sound of them clambering aboard. The Skipper didn't hesitate.

"Full ahead! Crash dive! Crash dive!" My last sight was of a shambling group of those things heading along the deck toward the tower, then the hatch clunked shut above me as I slid down the ladder into the control room. The boat tilted crazily as the prow went down, all of us stumbling around like drunk men. Then, a hideous rending sound as our port side made contact with part of the reef. For a terrible instant we wondered if the hull had been breached. But no, we continued our descent and escape. Minutes later, there was a collective sigh of relief as we hit open sea.

"Level out. Half ahead. Damage reports." the Skipper ordered as we fell back into our routines, the normalcy bringing some relief from our terrible experiences. It was then that Drexler called out. "Something approaching, sir, at speed."

"What is it, man?" I asked. "A ship? There are no screw noises."

"No, not a ship, sir," he replied. "It's a... well I don't know what it is but it is bearing down on us quickly."

"Action stations!" I cried. "Load aft torpedo tubes! Full ahead!"

The Skipper moved next to me and the crew gathered round, faces strained in the red light. The bubbling noise on the hydrophone grew louder, like nothing I had heard before, yet I knew what it was. One of the shore party, having also seen the thing, began to softly whimper. I cannot blame him. The Skipper had him quickly escorted to sick bay lest his panic infect the other men. The thing seemed to be gaining fast and I had that double horror; the U-boat man's primal fear of being crushed and killed in a narrow steel coffin. But also a deeper fear, a cosmic horror that, should I die at the hands of this thing, my soul might never know rest. I suddenly noticed my hands were shaking and I had begun to twitch. My self-examination was broken by the Skipper barking.

"Full spread, torpedoes los!"

At once the response came back as each tube was fired. Then came the desperate wait as our weapons sped their way through the inky blackness towards that terrible target. Would they harm it? Would they just pass through its viscous bulk? None of us knew,
all we could hear was the sound of the thing drawing closer, even above the sound of our own engines.

Six seconds, seven, eight, nine and no torpedo detonation! Damn, we had missed, or our weapons had passed through it! The noise now filled the control room and a voice shouted, "Brace for impact!" just before the boat juddered violently. I managed to remain on my feet only to be brought down by the second shaking. There was the loud sound of a nearby explosion, I was thrown across the room, my head impacted the periscope column and I knew no more.

I came to some time later on a bunk, the medic bending over me. I sat up but the world swam around, me so I sank back down.

"He'll live," grinned the Bones. "A nasty cut, mild concussion, perhaps, but he'll live."

The Skipper appeared over his shoulder. I rubbed my eyes

and asked him, "What happened? Are we safe?"

"It would seem so," replied the Skipper. "That thing had just reached us when one of the torpedoes exploded. I don't know how or why, maybe it got caught and carried in the thing. Whether the explosion killed it or just spread it far and wide, who can tell? All I know is that it is no longer pursuing us and we are heading back out to the ocean."

I sighed in relief and fell back into merciful unconsciousness.

I quickly resumed duties; there is little room for malingerers on a U-boat. We had, indeed made our way back out to deeper waters but had some serious problems. The structural damage caused by the creature and the explosion meant we would have to surface. Once we did, we discovered that the damage was not repairable except in a major port... and the closest friendly one lay on the other side of the Atlantic.

Later that day we went through Eisner's belongings, the Skipper taking charge of his effects. We agreed a story of Eisner being killed by the Ami locals. Kruger's sacrifice, we agreed, should be reported, for what good it might do anyone. The other things, that creature, those things in the sea... we never spoke about or even mentioned them again, it was as though we had never seen them. The log was completed in accordance with our story, not that it really mattered at that stage. The Skipper had changed. Always a dour man, I could see now a haunted look in his eyes. Perhaps he saw the same in mine. I tried to pretend, kid myself what we saw was some kind of mirage or delusion brought on by the stress of the situation. But there was no denying the huge gouge drawn along the side of the boat, or the foul, slimy substance around our props.

So it was that we stayed up on the surface. It was almost with relief that we were quickly picked up by an Ami destroyer, the *Vance* if my memory serves. The crew of that ship treated us well enough, we got a less friendly reception on landing. After being held at Portsmouth, we were transported down to Boston, where the whole crew was handcuffed and marched through the streets, the locals pelting us with garbage and insults. That was just a taste of what was to come. Our triumphal march ended at a large grey building, the Suffolk County Jail, I believe it was called. Once inside, we were given a going over by some real professionals.

Oh, they were Americans certainly but I'd seen enough Gestapo to know the type. They were very interested in any strange things we had seen and wanted precise information on locations. I got a bit roughed up but kept quiet, playing dumb and denying seeing anything other than some hostile locals. Others had it worse, the Skipper, for example. We later found out that he had died in his cell. Suicide, they said but that is nonsense, that was not the Skipper's way. He knew too much, that's what I think. He had Eisner's notes and knew things the Amis wanted kept quiet, so they killed him and made it look like he slashed his own wrists. That is my opinion and there's nothing can change it.

After that experience we were taken to a POW camp in the south. Eventually I was released and repatriated back to the Fatherland. I never settled back into normal life and drifted from job to job, flophouse to flophouse. These days I live in the south, close to the Swiss border, in the foothills of the Alps. I never want to go near the sea again.

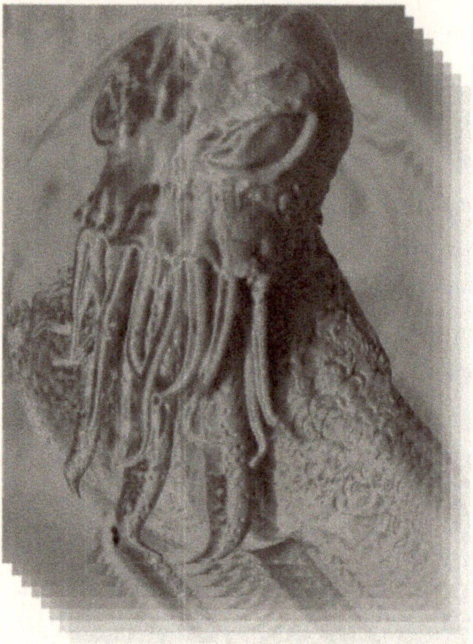

INNSMOUTH ACID

Tom had scored the acid after the Ultimate Spinach gig. He'd just come out of the Tea Party, the last strains of *Ballad of the Hip Death Goddess* ringing in his ears, the prismatic spray of the psychedelic light show burnt into his retinas. Tom flicked his dark, collar length hair back from his eyes, plucked his stripy t-shirt from his sweaty torso and slung his jean jacket over his shoulder. A long, lean figure, he began striding north along Berkeley, up towards the Common, back to the Beacon Hill apartment he shared with his wife, Sheila. She had stayed home that night, catching up on course prep for her job at Boston Uni. They had met at Harvard, Sheila studying law, Tom divinity and moved into the apartment just over a year ago, directly after getting hitched.

Nearing the top end of the street, Tom had paused in the warm August night air to light a Newport when a voice whispered to him from a nearby darkened doorway.

"Looking to score, mister?"

Tim was no stranger to the drug scene, acid in particular. He'd had his first experience with LSD as a grad student, in the tail end of the Marsh Chapel Experiments. After that, both he and Sheila had been regular attendees at Leary's Millbrook happenings until the increasing FBI raids put a stop to it all. To be honest, they both felt they had run their course with acid but Tom thought it might be fun to spike themselves one last time, see out the Summer of Love on a high. So he turned towards the figure in the shadows.

A hand reached out of the gloom and grasped Tom's arm; the hand looked flabby but had a surprisingly strong grip as it drew him in. Despite the warm evening, the figure was swathed in a heavy overcoat and a wide brimmed hat. Tom caught the glitter of eyes in a shadowed face and a fleeting glimpse of pale skin and a wide mouth. There was a faint odour about the man, somewhat masked by a strong cologne, that gave a hint of the sea. Well, Tom reasoned, the man didn't look like a narc.

"You got acid, man?" Tom asked.

The figure gave a short laugh. "Oh, yes. And potent it is, too."

"Really?" Tom regarded himself as something of a connoisseur. "What do you have? Owsley? White Lightning?"

"No," replied the man. "This is Innsmouth Acid."

"Innsmouth Acid?" Tom frowned, suspicion playing across his face. "I never heard of that before."

The dealer let out another wheezing laugh, "This is very new on the scene. It's made in a lab up north, on the coast. It's only just hit the streets."

Tom rubbed his chin, disengaging himself from the stranger's hold. "Hmm, I don't know, man. How do I know this is real gear?"

The man shuffled a little closer into the sodium glare of the street light and looked up into Tom's face.

"Oh this is real enough," he whispered. "I guarantee it will give you a Hell of a trip."

The next few minutes passed in a haze for Tom. He had a vague impression of the man's bulbous eyes peering into his, then came a sensation of slowly falling… no, not falling, sinking, into warm, bluey-green depths. A slow, comfortable descent, with a distant sound growing gradually louder. A piping flute, monotonous and atonal, yet curiously attractive. He felt the urge to surrender himself, to sink deeper… deeper…

With a start, Tom was back in the Boston street. The figure before him had retreated back into the shadow. Slightly unnerved, but putting it down to a flashback, Tom asked "How much?"

The figure put a hand inside the dirty coat and withdrew it, fingers curled shut.

"One sheet, five dollars." The fingers opened, revealing a folded sheet of paper. Tom drew close and prodded the edge of the paper with his finger, watching as it slowly uncurled. The blotter was covered in a design, which, on closer inspection, looked something like a squid head. There were a dozen tabs in all. Tom raised his eyebrows. What was five bucks?

"Okay, man. I'll take a sheet." They both moved closer into the doorway, the fishy smell stronger here, and the deal was done. Tom tucked the sheet away in his jacket pocket and was soon cutting across the Common on the way home.

Sheila was still up when he arrived back at their apartment, just finishing off her work. A petite redhead, with dazzling green eyes, she looked up and smiled as he came in the room.

"Good gig?"

"Yep, great." He returned her grin, dropping his jacket across the back of a chair, before going over to hug her. "I scored some acid too."

"Really? Cool. That'll be great for next weekend!"

Sheila mock-frowned at Tom's vacant expression and chuckled.

"You forgot, didn't you? We're heading to the beach with Ben and Angie. She's got the keys to her dad's place at Amity."

Tom smiled and kissed her forehead. "Yep, guess it slipped my mind but hey, now we can trip on the beach, watch the sunset, party a little, right?"

"Sounds good," replied Sheila, "Be a nice break before term starts again. Now, let me finish up here and I'll see you in bed mister... but take a shower first!"

The next Saturday, just after nine, Ben's VW camper honked outside the apartment and Tom and Sheila, a rucksack their only luggage, tripped down the steps and into the smoky interior. Angie, all frizzy hair and arm bangles, hugged them both. Blonde, bearded Ben peered over his raybans and gave them a big grin.

"All set for the trip, folks?"

"You bet," replied Sheila. "Speaking of which Tom scored some acid for us!"

Ben whooped and turned back to the wheel, hitting the dial on the radio and nudging out into the Saturday morning traffic. Soon they were out of Boston, heading south on Route Three.

It was a glorious August day. Angie lit up and passed around a joint and *Light My Fire* was blaring out of the radio. Windows down, the van sped along the Pilgrim's Highway, running parallel to the coast on their left. They stopped over in Plymouth for breakfast and just after noon, arrived at the ferry terminal in Falmouth.

The four of them drew in the fresh sea air that breezed through the van and soaked in the sights and sounds of the small coastal town. Gulls wheeled overhead, gathering in the wake of the small fishing boats returning to harbour with the morning's catch. The sea was a shimmering blue ribbon, sparkling under a cloudless sky. They all got the giggles as *Lucy in the Sky with Diamonds* came on the radio. After queuing for around fifteen minutes, the VW rolled forward onto the small Chappy Ferry and set off for the Island. It was a short crossing but a busy one, at this time of year the population of the Island could swell by as much as five thousand. Angie's family had owned a summerhouse here for years, a typical colonial style house with small lawn and white picket fence, within walking distance of the beach.

On the far side the van disembarked and Ben carefully picked his way through the pedestrians and cyclists, past the huge billboard on which a smiling bikini-clad bather on a float declared "Amity Island Welcomes You!". From there, he swung up onto the road that ran along the spine of the island. The summerhouse was at the far end, close to South Beach but before they got there Angie asked Ben to stop off at a place on Main Street, where she hired bicycles for them all.

"No one really drives here much," she explained as Tom helped her load the bikes into the back of the van. "The island's only about six miles long, much better to cycle!"

Soon after, they arrived at the summer house and were quickly unpacked and settled in. Taking the bikes, they headed back up the road to town, grabbing lunch at The Midway Grill and a few supplies at a nearby store. Dropping off bikes and shopping back at the house, they then took the short walk down to South Beach.

Bordered by small dunes, the soft, golden strand sloped gently down to the sea. The main beach area was crowded, mostly with families or groups of friends. Children splashed and screamed in the shallows, transistor radios blared tinny music, gulls cried and swooped on dropped popcorn, the gentle Atlantic waves hissed along the shore. A lifeguard sat in a small, wooden tower keeping careful watch, the air smelt of suntan lotion, ozone and fast food from the concessions along the promenade. There were signs for ice creams, candyfloss, fun floats and beach balls.

The four, now stripped down to shorts and bikinis, found a spot a short ways along and, throwing down towels, settled into the warm sand. Sheila rustled in her bag and produced sandwiches, Tom passed round a gourd of wine. Angie showed them a flyer she had picked up at the store.

"Check this out. The Ogres are playing tonight up at Beach Road. Shall we go?"

"Sure!" replied Ben. "Maybe we can drop Tom's acid before going? "

"Cool, man" grinned Tom. "Then after we can come down and party on the beach."

"Oh yeah," said Angie, motioning to the further end of the beach. "We'll head down to Cow Bay, there's usually a bonfire party going on. It'll be a blast!"

So it was, later that night, that the two couples were crammed together in the sweaty club, digging the sounds of the band. Just before leaving the house, Tom had taken the blotter sheet from the book he had hidden it in, smoothing it out on the kitchen table. Ben leaned over and squinted.

"What's that design, man? Looks like a squid head."

"I dunno, man." Tom shrugged. "The dealer dude said it's Innsmouth Acid, made some place up north."

"Innsmouth?" Angie frowned.

"You've heard of it?" asked Tom.

"Yep, I remember my Dad talking about it. He said his Pops was part of some team that investigated the place in the twenties. Apparently Pops was never the same after, ended up in an asylum. Dad said the Feds have continued to watch the place ever since, though he'd never been there."

Ben squirmed in his chair. He never did feel comfortable with the fact that Angie's old man was a Fed but Tom just laughed.

"Oh come on, Ange, you know how it works! The man will always invent scare stories, especially around acid. I'll bet those Innsmouth guys had some kind of arts and free love community going on up there way back then. You know, like the Bohos or the Beats. I bet the place was full of jazz dudes and bootleggers. Skat cats! A boobahdoobahdabbiwabbi..." He started miming playing a sax, Sheila joined in and soon the four of them were laughing and dancing around the kitchen. Angie picked up the large, kitchen scissors and lifted the blotter.

"So?" she snip-snipped the scissors. "How many tabs each?"

"Well, we don't know how strong it is," mused Ben. "But we're here for a few days. Let's do two each, we can always drop another one later on if we need too."

"Done!" Angie began cutting the blotter and dutifully handed out the sacrament.

A lazy grin spread across Tom's face as the band finished their version of *White Rabbit*. "Feed your head!" he sang with the rest of the crowd, hands thrust upwards in the smoky air. Strobe lights cut across his vision, fixing the dancers around him in monochrome, still frames, faces shining and beaming in the ecstasy of the moment. The acid was beginning to kick in, everything was fraying nicely around the edges. The bass was a pulse that mirrored his own, the guitar soared overhead, the fluting keyboard piped around the outskirts of his consciousness, calling something to mind that he couldn't quite remember. The moment was at once timeless and fleeting.

Sheila grabbed him and whooped, hair plastered over her sweat-streaked face. Laughing uncontrollably, she twined her arms around his neck and kissed him deeply. He closed his eyes and surrendered to the embrace, feeling his ego dissolving into hers, the two of them a bright, burning star in the centre of the universe.

Sheila slipped from his grasp and was swallowed up in the heaving crowd. The band were going into a new number, Tom didn't recognise this one. The drummer set a heavy, rhythmic pulse, the keyboard once again floating and ethereal over the top. Tom couldn't make out the words, the singer sounded harsh and guttural, where before he sounded sweet and light. It didn't even sound like English, there were too many consonants, the rest of the band joined in with a barking, croaking backing. The crowd seemed swept along with it, arms raised to the heavens at each chorus. "Ia! Ia! Ia!" they chanted.

The crowd looked different too. The beaming faces were still there but subtly changed. Certain proportions had altered, the figures looked squat, thickset. Mouths seemed wider, eyes bulged. The light show dimmed to give everything a violet-greenish glow that made Tom's head ache as the music increased in intensity. He put his hands to his head and screwed his eyes shut tight in an attempt to block out the strangeness.

When he opened them again, he saw with horror that the singer on the stage was pointing directly at him. All the faces in the club began turning to look and leer. Tom felt rooted to the spot as the faces drew closer, claw-like hands extending, reaching for him. With a gasp Tom realised they all had webbed fingers. Slit-like mouths opened to reveal short, serrated teeth, an odious stink washed over Tom, a smell of decay and rot.

The music built to a fever pitch as the hands reached him, grasping at his arms, his clothes, his hair. The strobe light kicked back in, Tom catching glimpses of even worse things in its flickering glow. Silhouettes of twisted, half human figures. The sudden flash of a sea-eaten face, dead eyed, skin shredded, seaweed entwined hair, crawling with crabs. An arm that reached for him ending not in a hand, but a lobster-like claw. Then, growing from the floor as if rising up from the ground before him, a dark, dark figure exuding menace and otherness. Up and up it rose to loom above him, a vague, amorphous bulk, a half glimpsed countenance with a horrible suggestion of mobility about its features.

Eyes of pale green balefire unaccountably drew him forward, towards the thing as it spread dripping arms... not to harm but to welcome and embrace him. With the last remnants of his awareness washing away like a sand castle before the tide, Tom fell into the dark embrace, feeling the clammy, whipcord like arms close around him, the stagnant, briny scent of the thing filling his nostrils, the sound of the eternal waves replacing the music in his ears.

"Tom! Tom!" He came to with a start. Sheila was holding him, looking up into his face with concern. Tom started and looked around. The original dancing crowd were back, the band was just coming to the end of *Little Red Rooster*. Tom staggered and rubbed his face. "I think I need some air." He held onto Sheila for support and they made for the exit, grabbing Ben and Angie on the way.

Outside Tom felt better, the warm night air calmed his nerves. Angie touched his arm with concern.

"Bad trip?"

Tom nodded. "I guess so. Wow, this stuff is stronger than I thought. How are you guys?"

Ben didn't answer, he stood grinning, pointing up at the stars that wheeled above. The sight broke them all into giggles and Angie suggested they head for the beach. The bike ride on acid was an experience, the whirr of the wheels combined with the whisper of the breeze. A station wagon passed as if in slow motion, its engine thrub-thrub-thrubbing, lit up like some kind of UFO.

On reaching Cow Bay they collapsed into giggles again, dropping the bikes in the dunes then running, whooping and laughing across the beach towards the sea. A little further along, a bonfire flamed, hurling fiery sparks high into the night sky. The strum of an acoustic guitar and the waft of sweet Mary Jane floated across the sand towards them but they took little notice. What had really caught their attention was the eternal sea.

Wordlessly they stripped, clothes dropped carelessly in a heap. As one they stepped forward, the cool surf washing smoothly over their feet.

No glance was shared, nothing was spoken, as if in telepathic communion the four all saw, all felt, all experienced the same thing. Before them, silver and black, swelled the untroubled surface of the Atlantic. Beneath a luminous full moon it lay, vast and ancient, its secrets hidden in icy depths. They all felt the pull of it, the desire to return to the primordial state, to the very source of existence. They felt the soft breeze reach out to caress their faces and bare shoulders. They felt the pull of the tide at their feet and ankles. The reflection of the moon promised a bright, shiny path out to the beyond.

And above it all, something else. A faint but unmistakable fluting, just on the edges of hearing, as though it were far away but, at the same time, very close. Growing more distinct and changing as it grew louder... not a flute but a voice, a female voice. Unlike any they'd heard before, unearthly in its tone and range. Soaring and dipping, pitching up and down like the waves, smooth but growing in its range, higher and lower. As if in answer, something out at sea changed; there was a movement in the stillness, a bubbling up, a rippling and spreading of waves.

The four stood, hand in hand, pupils dilated to the extreme, letting the sounds and sensations wash over them. Then came a deeper sound, a single pulse so low it was registered more in the viscera than the ears. Not so much a sound as a thought. A thought from somewhere far below, where sunlight never reached and blind creatures lived, fought, mated and died in eternal darkness. A thought that called to them, a thought that summoned them. As one, the four took a step forward.

The bubbling out at sea increased. There was another deep pulse, then again, repeated. With each increasing pulse, the four took a further step forwards. The world behind them had disappeared from memory, all that was important now lay before and beneath them. It was time to go home.

The Amity Gazette report August 31st 1967
Bizarre Suicide Pact?

The search continues for four young people missing believed drowned off the coast at Cow Bay. Eye witnesses in attendance at a nearby beach party, describe the group of four people walking hand-in-hand into the sea. "It was weird," said local resident Fred Griffen. "We saw them run down to the sea, strip off all their clothes, then slowly walk into the surf. We shouted out, but they just ignored us. By the time we ran over, they had gone!"

The four were believed to be tourists to the island but have yet to be formally named by the authorities. Police Chief Spivack told us, "This is a tragic incident and we are looking into all aspects of it. I ask anyone with information to come forward, even the smallest thing may be of assistance in our enquiries."

The Chief played down witness reports of people "seen swimming way out at sea" at the time as a trick of the light and also quashed any suggestion of shark attack. "That sort of thing doesn't happen in Amity!" he said. No bodies have yet been recovered. Police are continuing to investigate.

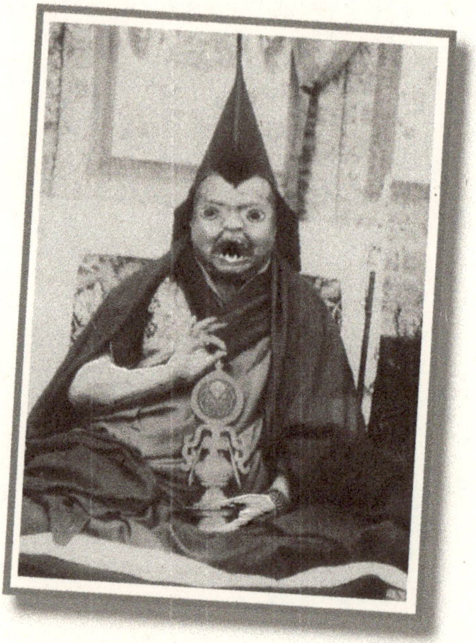

SHORE LEAVE

I first saw her at the Dragon, a dive just off the main stroll in Olongapo. Normally, we would wind up at Frank's but that evening I was late leaving the ship; I'd spent some time writing a letter to my wife. Any case, the huge bulk of the *Ticonderoga* behind me, I'd jumped into a cab and was soon walking the main drag. The ship was in dock at Subic Bay for minor repairs after combat operations in the Gulf of Tonkin. From there, we were to sail back home.

Home... It had been a rough tour. Seeing as how there'd be no flight deck operations for the foreseeable, I'd scored myself a shore pass for the duration.

It was humid as Hell, my crisp white shirt was already stuck to my back. I paused at a stall to buy some gum and a lighter, then saw a Lieutenant I knew from way back when, Joey Navinski from Illinois. We talked baseball over a Singapore Sling before he had to report back to base for his shift.

So I wandered the stroll aimlessly, curiously restless in the relentless heat. I was chowing down on some noodles on a corner when a sinuous thread of music caught my ears. I grabbed the thread and it led me down a side street to a bar I'd not seen before; the Dragon. Flickering neon, a young guy outside working the passing trade, a heavy on the door. The young guy grabbed my arm.

"Good show, sailor? You wanna see a good show?"

What the heck? I flicked him a bill and went in, the goon on the door nodding as I passed. If it was hot outside, it was sweltering inside. Typical dive, the bar running the length of one wall, the usual assortment of US personnel, locals and the odd tourist. Very odd, in one case, a bug-eyed character stood motionless at the bar. The slow moving ceiling fan did nothing to dispel the haze of sweat and smoke that filled the air. The music was coming somewhere from the back, I grabbed a cold beer from the barman and moved deeper in. At the rear of the room was a small stage with a DJ booth to one side. The music was odd, a local folk style maybe, all whining pipe and slightly out of tune chords on some kind of stringed instrument. Hendrix it wasn't.

That was when I first saw her.

Alone, on the stage, slowly swaying in time to the music, or at least, to what rhythm there was in that irregular pulse. Her eyes... that's what grabbed my attention first, staring, as though fixed on something or somewhere else. I'd seen the dead eyed stare in girls here before, of course, girls forced to do almost anything in order to feed their families. That stare wasn't so different from the eyes of many of our young men, also forced to do things they'd rather not. But this girl's look was different. There was a real absence of presence in that stare; like a shark aimlessly drifting in the sea, thinking nothing, not happy, not sad, just being.

Then the stare focused and fixed directly on me and that's

the moment I fell and fell hard, I swear it. She only held my gaze for a second or two before breaking it and continuing the dance. Lithe and supple, she glided around the cramped space, arms twining, hips gyrating. She wore a wrap-around ocean-blue sarong that occasionally revealed a flash of thigh. When she turned, most of her back was bare, covered in the most intricate tattoo I'd ever seen.

Entranced, I pushed forward through the crowd, as close to the stage as I could get. She saw me again. Was that a half smile on her lips? Another turn and I could see the tattoo more clearly. Silver and green, it shimmered across her shoulders and down her back. I've seen some good ink in my time but this was the work of a master. It looked like the skin itself was scaled and shining, iridescent in the glare of the stage lights.

The music reached a peak, then abruptly stopped and she was gone, through the curtained doorway at the side of the stage. The odd looking guy at the bar moved to the DJ booth, spoke to the man inside, then followed her though the curtain. Like a fish on a hook, I followed too but the bulk of another heavy loomed before me as I reached the door, holding up a warning palm and shaking his head. I retreated to the bar and ordered another beer. When the bottle arrived I rolled the ice-cold glass over my face before asking the barman, "That girl who just danced. Who is she?"

The man shrugged. "Don't know. First time I've seen her here." Then he was off serving a group of rowdy sailors at the other end of the bar. I hung around for another couple of hours, maybe she would do another show? But she never did. All that followed was the usual titty shakes and tired floor show. So, before midnight, I headed back to the ship.

Damn, that girl really got inside my head. I drifted in and out of sleep in the stifling heat of my cramped bunk. My dreams, when they came, were of that heart-shaped face, the long black hair, the glowing eyes... and that half smile, as though she were teasing me.

I had a few maintenance duties to perform the next day but couldn't fix my mind on anything. There were still two more nights on the pass, so I headed straight back to the Dragon after dinner. The place was as hot and sweaty as before. Two girls were on stage, working a double act, so I took up position close to the stage, called for a beer and waited. Sure enough, about an hour later she appeared, accompanied by the same strange looking man, who lurked again at the bar.

Did she catch my eye this time? Yes... and there was that subtle smirk again, I was sure of it. The music was a little wilder this time, her wrap-around a little looser, more flesh was on show. And more of the exquisite tattoo, that I could now see extended around one thigh. The routine ended as the night before, a sudden stop and she was through the curtain, accompanied by her chaperone.

I tried to follow again, flashing a few bills at the muscle on the door. No use. So I moved close and spoke in his ear, saying that I'd like to see the manager. He shrugged and motioned across the room. A boy of about fifteen hurried over and, after listening to the bouncer, grabbed my sleeve and told me to follow.

We went through an arch at the head of the bar and up a rickety flight of stairs. The boy knocked on the door at the top, opened it and beckoned me in. Inside, behind a desk covered with papers sat a Filipino man in his 50s, a cigarette glued to his bottom lip. He moved aside an overflowing ashtray and motioned for me to sit.

"I'm the manager, Hector Villarin. What may I do for you?"

"You have a new girl here, a dancer, the one with the tattoo. I'd like to speak to her," I explained.

I thought I saw a flicker of fear pass across Villarin's face. He peered over his glasses and replied, "I'm afraid that won't be possible. She is one of the new girls, I know her family. They brought her here and entrusted her to my care. But come now, sailor, we have plenty of other girls you can... talk to."

He smirked a little, maybe sensing my embarrassment; after all, I was a married man. What was I doing here thousands of miles from home chasing after a back-street bar dancer? I wiped the sweat from my eyes.

"No, you don't understand. It's that particular girl I need to speak to. You see, she likes me. I saw how she looked at me and - "

I broke off, both at the sound of my own voice and at the look on his face. Part sympathy, part contempt.

"I'll tell you what, sailor. How about we go down to the bar and get you a drink on the house? Then you can go back to your ship and then back to your country and your family. Best forget you ever saw that girl. Trust me."

He rose and I did the same, waving away the offer of a free drink. I stumbled back down the stairs and headed into the street. There was a dull ache behind my eyes but when I closed them, all I could see was that face. I slumped against the wall in the stinking alley rubbing a hand across my face. The sound of giggling straightened me up; two girls, the ones who had been onstage earlier, popped out of the door at the side of the building, walking past me towards the main street. I caught up to them in a few steps, grabbing one by the elbow, she span in alarm and I took a step back, raising my palms.

"Sorry, sorry! I didn't mean to frighten you. I just wanted to ask you something. Please, can you help me?"

The girl nodded to her friend and said something in Filipino. Her friend shrugged and replied, which I took as a yes.

"The other girl. The dancer who was on after you. Who is she? Where is she? How can I get to meet her?"

There was an exchange in Filipino again and the girl I'd grabbed answered.

"She's new. Don't know her name. But she come from Berja."

"Berja? Where is that?"

"Small village, north. Past Adams Beach, round the coast, by the mouth of the river."

"Thank you! Thank you very much."

Her friend let loose a torrent of words, accompanied by much arm waving. I looked at her, then questioningly back at the first girl.

"Is nothing," she answered. "We have to go now, bye, bye."

With that, the two disappeared into the crowd at the main strip and, nothing more to be gained, I returned to the *Ticonderoga* for another night of fitful sleep and feverish dreams.

My last day of leave, just one more chance to see her. But today I had a plan. No duties, so leaving the ship first thing I looked up my Lieutenant buddy and managed to loan a set of wheels off him; an Hodaka Ace 100, a neat little trail bike. Armed with an local map, I set off early, before the sun got too hot.

The roads were quiet as I whizzed along the main highway, shadowing the coastline to port. Stopping for a can of coke, I checked the map at a junction and took the left turn. This was no highway, it wasn't much more than a dirt track but it was leading towards the sea. I passed through a quiet village, nothing was moving except a few people working in the fields and a boy herding a reluctant pair of cows. None of them looked up as I passed. At the far edge of the village, an elderly lady stood in front of a roadside shrine. I pulled to a halt as she finished placing flowers in front of the statue of Mary. Crossing herself, she turned and I gave her my best smile, pointing to the map.

"Can you help me, ma'am? I'm looking for Berja."

The look on the woman's face changed immediately. She put one hand to her brow and placed the other on my arm.

"You should not go there, sir. There is nothing there for you."

"But I have to meet someone. You see, there is this girl..."

I trailed off as she stepped away from me, crossing herself once more, turning to hurry away. As she went she repeated. "Do not go there, sir, it is a bad place. Please, do not go."

Then she was away down the street and into one of the houses. I sighed and kicked the bike back into life. Guess I'd have to find it myself.

And find it I did, about an hour later. The track I was on devolved into a dirt path and I was glad I had the trail bike. This wound through low-lying salt marshes until I eventually came out onto a narrow beach. The track ran along the back of it and, ahead, I could see a collection of huts and small houses, not much more than shacks. There were a few fishing boats drawn up on the sand. The place was quiet as the grave, the only sound the gentle whisper of the sea. I puttered along the track until I came to the first of the houses. They were built along a narrow lane which I followed into the heart of the village.

There was not a soul in sight, though once or twice I thought I glimpsed a flicker of movement through a shuttered window. Not even a dog barked and the morning sun was relentless.

At the centre of the village I came upon an open square, with a temple stood in its centre. I put the bike on the stand and, removing my goggles, brushed myself down. As I did so, the door in the temple slowly creaked ajar. Taking this as an invitation, I trod up the shallow steps and went inside. The interior was shady and cool. Incense hung heavy in the air, masking an underlying sea odour. Light came from the glow of several large, black candles, fanned out on each side of a central altar. Atop the slab sat a squat figure, not the smiling Buddha you usually saw in this part of the world but something altogether more alien. The first trickle of fear ran down my spine.

Squat, as I've said and also squatting. A vaguely human shape but bloated in appearance. Tarnished and green it brooded, clawed feet clutching the edge of the altar as if for support. Folded wings jutted from the rounded shoulders and the head…. my God, the Head! A nightmarish mix of octopus and man. Tentacles sprouted from the lower half, almost seeming to writhe in the half light. Above them, two solid green eyes, some precious stones I imagined, twinkled with a malevolence unusual in a solid, static object. I say solid yet, despite its obvious solidity, the whole idol had a feeling of...flabbiness about it. Before I knew it I was stretching out a hand to touch it, God knows why! My motion was cut short by a soft voice behind me.

"Welcome to our temple. We get few visitors."

I spun round to see a short, local man dressed in purple monk's robes. His shaven head bobbed slightly as he spoke. I thought he must be blind, his eyes were pearlescent, yet he had no stick or cane. He grinned widely, revealing toothless gums. Judging from his mottled skin, he must be very old. I recovered my poise.

"I'm sorry, sir, I didn't mean to intrude. It's just that I came here... I'm looking for... well, you see.."

He raised a blotchy hand. "I know why you are here. Follow me, please."

He moved past me and I fell in behind, walking through an archway at the rear of the room and along a short corridor which ended in a closed door. He smiled up at me. This close to him, his body odour was somewhat overpowering but what he said next drove all thoughts of discomfort from my mind.

"That which you seek is within." With that, he turned and was gone. I nervously pushed the door open, onto a bare chamber that contained a round pool and an altar-like slab, similar to the one in the main room but mercifully bare of any idol. I moved forward, as if in a trance.

The pool in the centre of the room was about 15 feet across, with low steps leading down into it. The water within was green-tinged and murky, moving as if from some tidal flow. I walked around it towards the altar. At first I thought the altar was bare but, on closer inspection, I saw it was ringed with a frieze. Strange aquatic creatures, some humanoid in shape, some squid-like or shapeless, as well as more depictions of that unholy idol from the main room. I figured they must represent some old, local myth, though there was a curious familiarity at the back of my mind.

At once there was a sound and I turned to see her, beautiful and magnificent, emerging from the pool, striding up the steps like Venus arising from the sea. She glided towards me, that strange, half smile playing on her lips, her eyes drawing me into their sparkling green depths. Rivulets of salty brine ran down her bare shoulders, the wrap clung to her form like a second skin. Unspeaking, she extended a hand and I took it. Her touch was cold and slightly damp. With a curious detachment I noticed that her fingers were webbed. She led me to the altar and I took her in my arms, the wrap sliding wetly to the floor between us. Then I understood that the design on her back was not a tattoo.

When I came to again, I was sat on the motorbike at the dockside by the *Ticonderoga*. It loomed over me like some alien, cyclopean ruin. For a moment I was totally disorientated, with no memory of anything beyond that touch and the press of her cold lips against mine. Pulling myself together, I rode up the dock to return the bike to Navinski and after that was soon back on board ship.

The next few days passed in something of a haze. It was remarked on a few times by my fellow officers, but by the time we were back out at sea I'd returned to normal. Except for one thing. It began as a small itch on my lower back. I thought nothing of it at first but it persisted. Eventually, I managed to get time and space to take a look, with some twisting, in a mirror.

There, at the base of my spine... a small patch of grey green. At first I though it was nothing but a bruise, that somehow I'd knocked myself, nothing more. But the itching continued and the patch became more defined. The next time I looked, I could clearly make out the shape of scales. The colours had deepened too, becoming richer and slightly shiny. Like a tattoo. But tattoos don't spread and grow.

And now we are almost back at home port. Despite the warm weather, I've kept myself covered up, so no one has noticed my... change. My initial horror has subsided too, as though some deep part of me has been released and I carry within me the seeds of future growth.

I'm looking forward to seeing my wife when I get back to Boston. What wonderful things I will have to show her.

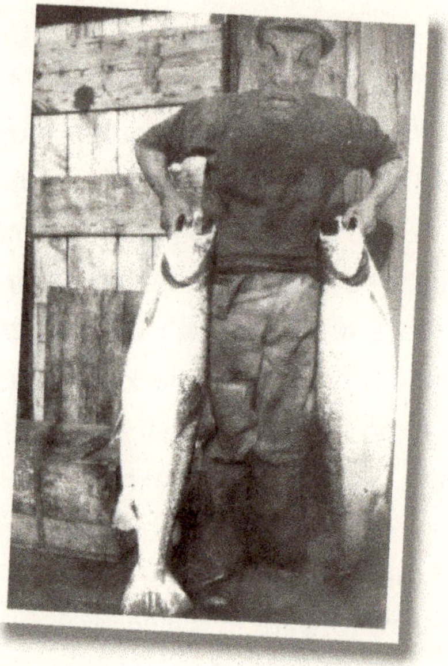

INNSMOUTH MARINA

Jimmy O'Brien nudged the nose of the BMW E30 over the ridge and got sight, at last, of his destination. Drawing to a halt on the pot-holed coastal road, he ran a hand through his gelled sandy hair, flicked open the Gucci briefcase on the passenger seat and took out the slim folder within. Leafing through it, he scanned the directions and checked the AAA map in his lap. The Manuxet River was ahead and to his right; definitely the correct place then, though curiously the town ahead was not shown on the map. Still, it had to be the place, there was no other south turn from Newburyport and the directions were quite clear. AAA or no, there was a town ahead, a dark smudge between the brown marsh and the grey sea. Innsmouth.

Shifting back into gear, Jimmy followed the road down from the hills and was soon enveloped in a flat landscape of reeds and sandbanks. The road narrowed, crumbling away at the edges. At one point Jimmy was so concerned about coming off the road that he slowed to a crawl and lowered his window to peer down and ahead. A shrill cry to his left brought him to a stop; for a crazy second he had the notion someone had called out his name from within the marsh. The notion was put to flight as a large tern lifted in a flutter and flurry of sound, flapping off into the clear, blue sky. Despite the warm sunshine Jimmy felt a slight shiver run through him. The chill breeze from the sea, no doubt, carrying with it the briny tang of rotting seaweed. He checked the directions again.

Until just recently Jimmy had never even heard of Innsmouth. Originally a New Yorker, he'd moved to Boston five years back in '79. After a couple of dead-end jobs, he'd joined The Hawkins Group, a smart new property development company overseeing projects up and down the coast. Exhibiting a flair for sales and presentations, Jimmy had rapidly risen up the ranks, taking over the running of the Newburyport office a month back. Now he was on a meet-and-greet trip for THG, following a call from Head Office. In fact the call came personally from the boss man Peter Hawkins himself, so Jimmy was only too pleased to jump to it.

There was a slim file titled *Innsmouth Marina*, left by his predecessor Ryan Field. It detailed how THG was considering the purchase of numerous properties in Innsmouth, with a view to constructing a new marina on the harbour. It had become fashionable for the young upwardly mobile to flock to the coast, either buying weekend retreats away from their city pads, or even looking for full time homes. THG had managed numerous similar projects, from the prestigious Seaport Hotel project in Boston, to the Hampton Beach Casino redevelopment up north. The town of Innsmouth was another dot that would help complete the aspirational living line now snaking along the New England seaboard.

Field had left the firm abruptly, under something of a cloud, according to Maggie the office manager. Drink and gambling, she was keen to tell everyone and anyone in a loud whisper, accompanied with a knowing nod, arms folded in disapproval. In any event, Field had gone, leaving a gap for Jimmy to move up and into. It had all been surprisingly easy, though Jimmy was never one to downplay his own talents. A formal interview with Hawkins and the senior partners, followed up by having Hawkins and his wife Kiri over for dinner one evening.

"We're a family firm," Hawkins had explained. "I like to meet the families of our main people. Gives me a sense of who they are. Family is everything, don't you think?"

Jimmy had nodded enthusiastically in agreement. Hell, for the wage rise he was looking at, he'd have sat up and begged. Jackie had been fine with it; the kids, well Travis was seven and Lauren only four. They didn't really know what was going on but they had all made a good impression on the Hawkins. Following that, the promotion was a shoe-in, Jimmy got the Newburyport office and felt he was on–track at last

Swearing under his breath, Jimmy tossed the folder aside and cursed his predecessor. Aside from a glossy THG brochure, the folder held just two sheets of foolscap about Innsmouth, the first comprising a set of directions and a few scribbled notes from Field mentioning "sullen and uncooperative locals."

The name of the current Mayor topped the second sheet, under which was a brief history of the town. An out of the way, clapped out fishing town was the long and short of it;

the most exciting event was a Fed raid on bootleggers operating out of the place in the Twenties. Since then it had been largely abandoned, industry gone, fishing fleet in decline; in other words, cheap properties ripe for development. If a few diehards still remained, the promise of a large cheque or a compulsory purchase order would soon have them shifted. There was no stopping progress; especially the progress of Jimmy's career. Wrapping up this deal might put him on the first steps to a partnership ...

Hills filling his rear view mirror, nothing but the ribbon of the marsh road ahead, Jimmy drove on. His daydreams were brought to earth with a bump as the town came into sharper view. Shit, who in their right mind would want to live here? First there was the stench. Strong enough in the marsh, it now permeated the interior of the BMW and Jimmy raised the window and flicked the AC into full operation. The reek blew across from the harbour just visible to the left, smelling as though a huge pile of fish had been dumped there and left to rot in the hot sun.

Next were the houses; tumbledown, derelict, waist high weeds pushing through the cracked sidewalks, windows empty and dark. Jimmy thought he caught a glimpse of a pale face at one, on second glance it was just a flap of rag caught in the soft breeze. Pressing on, the purr of the engine the only sound in the empty streets, Jimmy was soon enclosed in the narrow turns of the old town. The houses became larger but there was little improvement in condition; and still he had not seen a living soul. Run down? The place looked like a ghost town.

As he drove on, Jimmy felt he was travelling along the floor of a canyon. The decaying houses loomed over the cramped streets, the midday sun doing nothing to dispel the sombre shadows to either side. He became a little disorientated, eventually rumbling across a thin bridge, the roar of the Manuxet falls just audible below. Turning left, he followed the riverside road and, finding himself in a town square, pulled to a halt at the kerbside. The buildings here were in a better state of repair but obviously hadn't been decorated for years. The green-painted window sills reminded him of his Grandparent's house as a child. Probably lead paint; he shook his head. Still, it should all make it easier to move any existing tenants out. The prospect of a room in a modern retirement home surely had to be a welcome proposition to any old timers still living here, even the stubborn ones.

At last, he caught sight of life. Outside a store, a hunched figure ran a broom half-heartedly across the sidewalk. Jimmy threw his filofax and Motorola cell phone into the briefcase, kept the folder in his hand and got out of the car. Taking the Ralph Laruen jacket from the rear seat hanger, he slid into it and shut the car door with a satisfying thunk. Dialling in his finest *I'm your new best friend* smile, he straightened his tie and made for the figure.

"Hi there!" he called from about ten feet away. No response. Jimmy frowned and moved closer, trying again. "I said, hi there!" Still no response, the figure remained turned away, engrossed in the sweeping. Jimmy took a couple more paces forward and placed a hand on the man's shoulder. The broom clattered to the ground as the figure turned, arms flying up in a protective flinch, causing Jimmy to instinctively snatch back his hand. The young man before him worked his jaw soundlessly, face rigid in fear. Drool ran from his lips and the man's eyes positively bulged in their sockets. Cowering, he backed rapidly away, disappearing into the gloom of the store.

"Pay no heed to Nathan," said a voice behind him. Jimmy span to face the newcomer. "He's daft as that brush and deaf as a post."

Jimmy recovered his composure and smile, extending a hand to the elderly man who shuffled toward him. "Good day to you, sir! Jimmy O'Brien. Pleased to meet you."

The man wiped a hand on the seat of his coveralls and grasped the proffered hand in a surprisingly strong grip. Jimmy tried not to wince.

"Frederick Eliot. Well we don't get so many visitors here, what might yer business be, Jimmy?"

Jimmy maintained the smile and wriggled his slightly numbed fingers. Reaching into his jacket he withdrew a business card, passing it to Eliot. The old timer smiled, revealing small, yellowed teeth. Now he looked at the man closer, Jimmy found something disquieting about the man's appearance. He couldn't pin it down to a single feature, more a combination of things. There was his skin, some condition perhaps, flaky and peeling heavily across the scalp. Added to that was the body odour, though perhaps that came from the man's darkly-stained overalls. No, it was more than that, something about the man's posture and movement. It seemed curiously fluid, though his grip had been like iron.

"I represent The Hawkins Group property developers. I'm here to meet with the Mayor, regarding potential redevelopment of your harbour area." Jimmy's eyes gleamed with evangelical passion as he flicked open the folder, revealing the brochure, displaying one of the artist mock-ups of a new marina.

"Just imagine, sir, this whole town revived! A marina, luxury flats overlooking the harbour. A coffee shop here in the town square. Some smart bars and eateries, maybe a shopping mall, perhaps a luxury car dealership?"

Eliot's response was to double over with a gurgling laugh. Jimmy's distaste for the man grew stronger.

"Have it all figgered out don't ya, son?" Eliot turned to shuffle off, calling over his shoulder, "Good luck with that. You'll find us Innsmouth folk like things the way they are."

With that, the man was gone. Jimmy noticed his card now lay on the sidewalk. Shaking his head, he checking the contents of the folder again. He had the Mayor's name, Marsh, but no clue as to his whereabouts. He turned back towards the store, planning on asking the owner the location of the Mayor's office but the door was now shut, a closed sign dangling against the grimy glass. He thought he caught a glimpse of movement within, a pasty face briefly emerging from the gloom. The idiot again? Perhaps. Not a problem, Jimmy would find someone else to ask. After all, getting to know the locals was part of the mission.

Jimmy walked over to the tall, imposing building across the square. The dusty sign proclaimed *Gilman Hotel*, its windows were grimy, the net curtains behind them yellowed and torn in places. Mustering up his smile once more, Jimmy trod the steps and pushed the heavy door open. Inside was a spacious reception area, with a couple of archways and a large staircase leading off. The place smelled damp and looked neglected, the carpet worn, the green wallpaper stained and peeling in places. From somewhere, an unseen record player languidly crackled out an old Thirties jazz tune. Behind the desk stood a solitary figure, another elderly man, stooped, reading a newspaper. The man's lips moved as he read. At Jimmy's approach, the desk clerk peered at him over half rim specs with prominent, watery eyes.

"*Shit,*" thought Jimmy, "*does everyone in this place have some kind of condition?*" However, his smile never wavered.

"Good day, sir. My name is Jimmy O'Brien. Do you know where I might find the Mayor's office?"

The clerk regarded Jimmy unblinking. Then, in a croaky voice he asked, "You need a room?"

Jimmy's smile flickered slightly. "No, sir. I'm looking for the Mayor. Do you know where his office is? Mayor Marsh?"

The clerk blinked slowly, as if digesting this new information, then croaked again, "Mayor not here. We have rooms, though. You need a room?"

Jimmy's smile was replaced by a scowl and he swore under his breath, thinking *is this guy for real or is he jerking my chain?* Either way, Jimmy spun on his heel and exited the hotel, only to swear again. A small crowd had gathered round the BMW, about a dozen men, all elderly. Some were touching the vehicle, one had opened the door and was peering inside.

"Hey! Hey!" Jimmy strode across the street, waving the folder. "Get away from there. You never seen a car before?"

As one, the group turned to silently stare at the stranger. Jimmy flinched; most of the group had even worse physical abnormalities than he'd already seen. Mottled skin, bulging eyes, strangely shaped heads topped with wispy hair. Two looked to have hunchbacks, so twisted over were they. Jimmy drew himself up to his full six foot two and marched to the car, the group scattering slowly on his approach.

"You'll have to excuse them," floated a feminine voice from a nearby doorway. "We get so few visitors these days."

Jimmy turned at the sound, his smile reappearing in a flash as he took in the woman who had spoken. In her twenties, he estimated, quite tall, curvaceous. Long black hair tumbled over her shoulders, framing a pale, pretty face. She wore black pants and a green shirt that matched her eyes. Jimmy virtually skipped over the sidewalk to shake her hand.

"Jimmy O'Brien. I'm looking for the Mayor, do you know where his office is?"

"Sonia Marsh. I certainly do, the Mayor is my Uncle. I'll take you there. It's not far, we can walk."

Jimmy nodded and turned to secure his car. The group flinched as the central locking clicked in and the indicators flashed.

"No need to lock it, there's no crime in Innsmouth." Sonia moved to his side.

Jimmy nodded again and reminded himself to dial down the smile; he didn't want to come across as a grinning idiot. Putting on his serious business face, he waved a hand, "After you, Miss."

They walked for around ten minutes, the scenery doing nothing to dispel Jimmy's earlier assessment of the place. On the way he chatted breezily to his guide, learning that she had been born in Innsmouth and was not long back after studying law at Miskatonic Uni in Arkham. She had returned to help run the family business.

"My parents are getting old," she explained. "They will

be going soon. I have to be prepared for when they are no longer around."

Jimmy smiled politely, thinking this was a rather odd way to talk about the demise of one's parents. He put it down to New England pragmatism. By then they had walked across the main Manuxet Bridge; a block or two on brought them into another open space, with streets radiating away from the unkempt, circular green at its centre. Jimmy was struck again by the quietness of the place. The only other people he'd seen were furtive figures half glimpsed down narrow side streets that were hemmed in by the tall, gambrel houses that lined them. There was no rumble of traffic, no bark of a dog, no sounds of children playing.

He remarked on this to his guide but she merely shrugged and continued on. They crossed the green by way of an overgrown path. A briar caught at Jimmy and he frowned in irritation as it snagged his suit pants. As he bent to release himself he caught a glimpse of something scuttling away into the undergrowth. A rat? That kind of size; but this thing moved more like a crab, there had been an unpleasant suggestion of too many legs.

Jimmy straightened up sharply, Sonia was waiting ahead. At the far end of the path she pointed to the stone building ahead, an old Gothic-style church from the look of it. Shabby and grey, the clock face on its tower had no hands; closed, peeling shutters ran along each side, though the main entrance lay open and a figure in a baggy suit appeared in the doorway. Sonia waved to the figure and turned to Jimmy.

"That's my Uncle, the Mayor. Well, I'd best be getting back. Good luck, Mr O'Brien."

"Thanks for your help, Sonia. And please, it's Jimmy." He gave his most charming smile and watched in appreciation as Sonia walked back across the green. Then, professional once more, he crossed the street and bounded up the steps, hand outstretched, to meet the Mayor.

Mayor Marsh exhibited many of the characteristics Jimmy had already seen in local residents; the large eyes, the flaky skin, the sparse, lank hair. Yet he greeted Jimmy warmly and bade him enter. On the way to his office, Marsh explained that the old Congregational church had been converted some years back for use as a Town Hall. The original Town Hall, he explained, had been largely destroyed in the troubles in the Twenties. By then they had reached the Mayor's office and Jimmy took the seat before the large desk.

"The troubles? Bootleggers, wasn't it? A raid by the FBI, I think I read?"

Marsh gave a small cough and briefly tugged at the collar of his shirt. "Well, that's all long in the past. It is the future you are here about according to the telephone call from Mr Hawkins, am I correct?"

"Indeed, sir. As you may know, we at THG have already been involved in a number of prestigious developments all along the Massachusetts coast." He opened the folder and slid the THG brochure across the desk. Marsh reached out to pick it up. As he did so Jimmy noticed, with some distaste, the slight webbing between the man's fingers. Marsh scanned the brochure briefly and smiled.

"Yes, I see. I'll be blunt, Mr O'Brien. Innsmouth is dying. What you see around you now was once a thriving seaport. Fishing and boat building initially, though my own ancestors, Captain Obed Marsh in particular, began a thriving import business, most notably in gold. But the old refinery has been quiet for years now and even our fishing trade is but a shadow of its former self."

The Mayor touched a hand to his collar again, drawing Jimmy's attention to the curious folds of skin peeking above it. He wouldn't be surprised if the local ailments were a result of the obviously unsanitary living conditions in this stinking place. But he put such thoughts aside and, engaging his best professional manner, continued his patter.

"All the more reason, sir, for carefully considering THG's proposals. We can transform your town into a thriving seaside haven that young professionals and families will flock to. Now, of course, everything is subject to surveys and architect's reports but imagine... Innsmouth Marina! A rejuvenated harbour, seafront hotels, smart restaurants, weekend holiday homes and the like." Jimmy stood now, warming to his subject, hoping to infect Marsh with his enthusiasm. "That, in turn, will generate jobs for your youngsters and bring new people into the area, thus benefiting the local economy."

Marsh stared up, unblinking at the young man and gave a wide smile.

"I'm afraid we don't have so many young people in Innsmouth, Mr O'Brien. As you may have seen, our population is an ageing one. And with every passing year, more of the old ones leave us. Soon... soon it will be my turn."

The Mayor rubbed at his neck again and Jimmy wondered

if the old man had some kind of disease, perhaps? He was about to enter Phase Two of his pitch when the Mayor abruptly stood.

"Mr O'Brien, Innsmouth is in desperate need of fresh blood. More than ever, we need young people here, the town will die without new life. If sacrifices need to be made to continue our existence, then so be it. Of course, the town elders will need to be consulted."

"Of course, of course, yes sacrifices for progress are a good thing," Jimmy nodded seriously. In his head he was high fiving himself, thinking of the huge bonus he'd be earning off the back of such a large deal. He beamed again. "If there is any way I can help, I'd be happy to meet with the elders. That would be in a council meeting, I take it?"

Marsh smiled again and placed a firm hand on the younger man's shoulder. "Yes, you could call it that. In any event, let us stay in touch and begin moving ahead with plans."

He guided Jimmy back out onto the steps. Blinking in the afternoon sun, Jimmy noticed, for the first time, the building on the opposite side of the green. If nothing else, it stood out for its cleanliness compared to the rest of the town. White stone pillars in classic Georgian style, supported a large portico, on which some insignia was engraved that Jimmy couldn't quite make out from this distance. He turned to Marsh, who was blinking in the bright sunlight and asked.

"What's that place? Looks like a classic Masonic building."

Marsh shaded his eyes with a spotted hand and nodded.

"That was its original purpose, I believe. These days it is used as a meeting house and place of worship for local people."

Jimmy raised his eyebrows. "Place of worship? Why not use the church here?"

Marsh began to chuckle, a curiously wet sound that again brought the thought of disease to Jimmy's mind.

"We have our own ways here in Innsmouth, Mr O'Brien. Now, I have some things to attend to. Are you able to find your way back to your vehicle?"

The young man nodded in the affirmative and set back off across the green. Turning briefly, he saw Marsh motionless in the shadowed doorway, staring at him without expression before retreating slowly into the dark interior. Jimmy took a closer look at the building opposite as he approached it. The carving on the portico revealed itself as a weird, unfamiliar design. Centred around an eye, sinuous tentacles writhed out to the edge of the triangle. Humanoid figures were carved along the base, though possessed of curious features, hunched with almost fish-like features. Despite the warmth of the sun, Jimmy felt a chill run through him, as if some deep ancestral memory had been touched.

As he drew level with the building Jimmy noticed a side door was open, a black void in the white exterior. His eye was further drawn by the flicker of motion. A figure clad in a dark red robe traversed the doorway, being briefly illumined by the bright sunshine. It was a momentary glimpse but Jimmy had an uneasy impression of a twisted, deformed shape beneath the robe. Its undulating locomotion seemed more animal than human but, in an instant, it was gone and a slightly shaken Jimmy resumed his walk back to the car.

The day was still hot and, business done, Jimmy had removed his jacket and loosened his tie by the time he reached the BMW. The place was still deserted, the only sound the distant whisper of the falls and the cries of gulls from the harbour. Jimmy put his jacket back on and was fishing in his pockets for the keys when he noticed, with annoyance, that two of the car tyres were flat.

"Shit!" he squatted down on the sidewalk. Both tyres on this side were pancakes. Jimmy looked around, in vain, for broken glass, or nails or some similar cause. Nothing. On closer inspection, he found what looked like slash or stab marks on the tyres; deliberate, then! He might blame local kids but there didn't seem to be any. But why would the old timers do this? Jealousy, perhaps?

He unlocked the car and took out his briefcase. Setting it on the roof of the car, he flipped it open, took out the Motorola, pulled out the aerial and made to dial. Then he paused. Who should he call, the local cops or the AAA? He figured the cops could do little and it would hardly be the crime of the century in their book. No, he would call the AAA first; they could get him out of this place, then he would consider reporting the vandalism. Pressing the buttons, though, he was dismayed to find no signal. Shouldn't be surprising in this backwater, he figured. He put the phone back in the case and turned to the store. Surely they had a phone? But the closed sign was still in place and tapping on the glass brought no response.

The hotel, then! Growing more irate by the second, Jimmy bounded up the steps. What sounded like the same jazz tune echoed through the room, the same clerk was in place, reading the same newspaper. He glanced again over the top of his specs.

"Do you have a phone I can use?" Jimmy snapped.

The clerk nodded, reaching under the desk and bringing out a piece of apparatus that looked like a prop from a 50's movie. Checking the number from a card in his wallet, Jimmy rang the AAA. Nothing. The line was dead. The clerk had returned to scanning his newspaper.

"How do I get an outside line?" Jimmy asked, loosening his tie further.

"Ain't no outside line," the clerk slowly answered. "Phone here's for local calls only."

"Fuck's sake!" Jimmy ran a hand over his brow, then took a breath. "Alright. Okay. Is there such a thing as a local garage in this place? Someone who can fix flat tyres?"

"I'll call Joe Pierce." The clerk nodded with a wide grin and took the phone from Jimmy. Dialling with a white, sausage-like finger, he spoke quietly into the receiver. Replacing it in the cradle, he turned back to Jimmy. "Be here'n ten minutes. Need a room?"

Jimmy shook his head. "Thank you. No, I don't need a room. I'll wait outside."

Returning to the car, he removed his tie and returned his jacket to the rear hanger. Suddenly feeling thirsty and hungry, Jimmy realised that Marsh hadn't offered him so much as a coffee. He decided to wait in the car, letting down the windows to allow in what slight breeze there was. Sure enough, fifteen minutes later a battered panel van rolled into the square. A figure in oil-stained overalls exited the cab and limped over to the BMW. The man leaned in, his face uncomfortably close to Jimmy, who couldn't help but recoil at the man's appearance and odour.

"Got trouble, son?" the mechanic, presumably Joe Pierce, asked?

"Yes, thank you, yes." Jimmy got out and showed the man the problem. Pierce stood, chin in hand, apparently deep in thought.

"It's a smart vehicle you have there, mister. New model, right?"

Jimmy nodded, "Yes, it's a company car, the latest Beamer. Central locking, CD player, air con, six cylinders. It really does move."

Pierce pulled a face."But not without tyres."

Jimmy struggled to remain polite. "Exactly. Can you replace them?"

"That I can," Pierce replied. Jimmy sighed in relief but Pierce continued, "Will take a couple of days though. Don't have nothing like these in the garage. Will have to send to Ipswich for 'em, I reckon."

"A couple of days? Jesus!" Jimmy felt the beginnings of a headache dully throb behind his eyes. He squeezed them tightly shut then opened them again. "How about a tow truck? Could you tow me back to Newburyport?"

Pierce smiled and shook his head. "It's out of action at the moment. Manifold blew last week. Difficult to get the parts out here, see?" With that he began limping back to his van, his parting shot over his shoulder was, "Reckon you'd be best shacking up in the hotel there. I'll order the tyres, a day or so and you'll be off away. I'll come back here once I have 'em."

With that, the mechanic was gone. Jimmy slapped the BMW roof in frustration. It would have to be the hotel, then. Work was not a problem, after all he was where he was supposed to be. But he was unhappy at not being able to let Jackie know the situation. He'd have to see if there was some way of getting a message to her, surely someone in this dump had communication with the outside world. Grabbing his jacket from the car, he returned to the hotel. The clerk, newspaper now folded on the desk, him, looked up.

"Can I help you, sir?" he smirked.

Jimmy sighed. "Yes, I need a room."

The clerk dragged a heavy book across the counter and spun it around.

"It's $20 a night. Please sign here, sir."

As Jimmy signed he noticed the previous entry was for two years ago. How on earth did this place stay open? Duly signed, he dropped a twenty from his wallet and returned book and pen to the clerk, who slid a large, old fashioned key across the dusty counter.

"Room 305. There's a shared bathroom just along the corridor."

Jimmy accepted the key with a resigned shrug. "Is there anywhere I can get some food around here? Any restaurants?"

The clerk sniggered as if at some private joke. "I guess so. There's the Manuxet Cafe, opens at seven most nights. Turn right, just across the way."

Jimmy thanked him and took the stairs to his room. The decor didn't improve at all. If anything, it was worse on the upper floors. The stairway and corridors were dim, with an occasional bare bulb. The wallpaper had seen better days and the carpet was uncomfortably soft under foot, not the lushness of a new carpet but more spongy, like stepping onto fungus. The faint echo of that old jazz-age tune wandered up the stairs and followed him along the corridor like a ghost.

Room 305 was halfway along, Jimmy slid the key into the lock, turned and had to push the door hard to get it open. A vaguely damp smell wafted out of the opening. Inside was a room that could only be described as sparse; an iron-framed bed with a lime green quilt, an old wardrobe with one door hanging half open and a bedside cabinet. The carpet felt damp underfoot and there was a large patterned patch on the wall which Jimmy couldn't quite work out was modern art or mould. Placing his briefcase on the floor, he sat heavily on the bed, which creaked alarmingly under his weight, and idly opened the cabinet draw. Empty, apart from some dust bunnies; not even a Gideon bible. He sighed. There seemed little point in asking for another room, he imagined they were all like this.

Standing, he moved over to the sole window in the room. Through the dirty nets he had a view of the square below, his car outside the store. Hanging his jacket in the wardrobe, he rolled up his shirtsleeves and went in search of the bathroom. He found it at the far end of the corridor, a tiled room containing a grimy bath tub and sink, a fly-specked mirror and a toilet. After using the toilet, which gurgled alarmingly when he flushed it, Jimmy ran the faucet to wash his hands and face. There was a distant knocking, followed by an explosive spurt of tepid, brown water. Jimmy reeled back, gagging at the stench.

Desperate for air, he moved to the frosted glass window

above the john and, standing on the bowl, managed to open it with a hard tug. Taking a few breaths, he returned to his room. Glancing at his his Rolex, he saw there were a couple of hours yet to kill before the cafe opened. Jimmy checked the Motorola again, but still no signal. Resigned, he decided to take a nap before heading out to eat. Placing the Rolex face forward on the cabinet, he settled back on the bed, reluctantly resting his head on the greasy pillow.

A sound awoke him. It took him a moment to remember where he was. Then he heard the sound again, a shuffling noise, as though something was being dragged along the corridor outside. Jimmy rose quietly from the bed and moved to the door. Placing his ear against it, he heard the scuffling draw near, until it was right outside his room. Then there was silence. He became aware of a stench in the air, that seaweed rot smell once more. It brought a feeling of dread, though why that might be, Jimmy could not say.

He found himself holding his breath, straining to hear any more noise from outside. Then he heard it... a curious breathing... wheezing and wet, as if from disease ravaged lungs. It came directly from the other side of the door and Jimmy had a vague impression of a presence there, crouched, listening as he was listening. Jimmy glanced down as a movement caught his eye, watching with horror as the door knob slowly rotated. Swiftly and smoothly, he reached down, turning the heavy key with a solid click. Immediately the doorknob returned to its original position. There was a tense silence, then the shuffling began once more, moving away, back along the corridor.

The curious incident had taken only a couple of minutes

but Jimmy' shirt was soaked with sweat. He let out a long breath and slumped against the door panels. His hands were shaking slightly. After a couple of minutes he pulled himself together and, unlocking the door, peered out into the corridor. Empty; though even more gloomy now that evening had come. Jimmy retreated to his room, picking up his watch and noticing it was seven-thirty. His stomach rumbled as if in reminder and, grabbing his phone and jacket, he made his way downstairs. The clerk was not in place, the whole building seemed deserted. Even the music had stopped. Stepping out, he was gratified to see lights on at the cafe. At last, a sign of normal life.

Jimmy crossed the street and pushed open the door, the few heads inside the room swivelling at his entrance. The place was what you'd call *homely,* he guessed, a far cry from the fashionable eateries he was used to dining at. Seating himself at a table near the window, he ran an eye over the menu. It didn't take long, there wasn't a lot of choice; almost entirely seafood. An elderly lady, exhibiting many of the characteristics of what Jimmy had come to think of as "the Innsmouth look" came to take his order. He ordered a bowl of chowder with fresh bread and a carafe of water.

While waiting, he checked for a phone signal once again. Still nothing. When the meal arrived he fell to with gusto, even the slightly unusual flavour of the chowder doing nothing to discourage his appetite. He was just finishing when a familiar voice interrupted his repast. It was Sonia Marsh and he bade her sit and join him. She signalled to the waitress and sat with a smile.

"Are you enjoying our town so much you can't leave, Mr

O'Brien?"

"Something like that," he grinned. "And, please, it's Jimmy."

The waitress cleared the table and brought over coffees as Jimmy told Sonia of his predicament. Sonia was an easy listener, laughing at his jokes and, as they chatted, Jimmy found himself becoming more and more attracted to her. There was something slightly odd about her, an indefinable quality but that only added to her allure. At one point their hands brushed across the table and Jimmy glanced up full into those deep, green eyes. They seemed to pull him in and hold him. There was a promise there...

With an effort Jimmy glanced away. What was he thinking? Jackie would be worried sick about him at this very moment and here he was, flirting with some country girl. If Sonia noticed any sign of his guilt, she made no show of it. In fact, she turned away as a man came into the cafe and walked over to their table, bending to whisper in her ear. She nodded and the man left.

"Problem?" asked Jimmy.

"Nothing I can't handle," she smiled. "But I do have to go. I have some things to prepare."

"Aww, do you have to go so soon?" asked Jimmy. "I was enjoying our chat."

Sonia pouted. "I do. But tell you what, how about a drink before I go?"

"Sounds good!" Jimmy beamed. "But I didn't notice any alcohol on the menu."

"Leave it to me. Locals get local rum punch! I'll order us a shot each." She scraped her chair back and walked over to talk to the waitress at the counter. Sure enough, a couple of minutes later, two tankards were placed before them. Jimmy lifted his, taking in the heady aroma.

"Spiced rum punch," Sonia told him. "A local tradition. Bottoms up!" Together they upended and drained the tankards. Jimmy coughing as the fiery liquid passed down his gullet. Sonia gave a delightful laugh.

"And now I really must go. I'll pop into the hotel tomorrow, if you like? Perhaps show you the local sights?"

"That would be nice." Jimmy stood and put on his jacket, leaving a few bills on the table. He moved to the door, holding it open as Sonia glided past, giving him a peck on the cheek before disappearing into the night. Jimmy sighed heavily and made his way back to the hotel.

No clerk again but the key was heavy in his pocket as he climbed the stairs to his room. Halfway up he began feeling dizzy. That local rum was obviously potent stuff. By the time he reached his room, everything was blurring at the edges and swimming slightly. Not even bothering to remove his jacket, with a soft sigh, he fell back on the bed and sank into darkness.

Jimmy was suddenly awoken again. Not by noise this time, but by pain, a sharp, stabbing pain in the guts. His head was pounding too and he felt hot. Groggily, he sat up and stumbled to the window. Grabbing the sash, he tried to lift it, wanting to let some air into the humid room but the window stayed resolutely shut. Rubbing a hand across his eyes, Jimmy glanced out through the nets. There was a figure in the square below, stood beside the old street lamp. Despite the warm night, it wore a large coat and hat, under which no features could be seen. But Jimmy had the strange impression that man was looking up at the window and drew back with a gasp. As he did so, a second, then third figure slid into the glow of the street lamp. Again, no features were visible at this distance but there was hint of strangeness in the posture of each and the way they moved.

Jimmy's guts spasmed again, sending him reeling for the door and hurtling down the corridor, hand on the wall for support. He made the john just in time, lifting the lid and heaving violently into the cracked and stained bowl. For minutes he knelt there as the spasms jetted the vomit from his nose and mouth. Slowly the convulsions subsided and Jimmy sat, back resting against the bath, breath coming in gasps. Not daring to look at the regurgitated chowder inside, he closed the toilet lid and used it as support to rise unsteadily to his feet.

He was about to pull the chain when a sound caught his ear. Gruff voices. He thanked God he hadn't had time to turn on the bathroom light and, opening the door a crack, peered down the corridor. There, outside his room... three figures, the ones from the street by the looks of it. They were huddled as if in conference, one speaking in a low, croaky voice. The words were indistinct but their intentions became clear as, with a shout, the three of them burst into the room.

Not stopping to think, Jimmy closed the bathroom door and shot the bolt into place. Shit! What was happening? What did they want? To rob him? He hardly had any cash on him and just the one credit card. Were they after the car? The keys were in his jacket pocket, which he was still wearing, he realised he hadn't even taken it off before crashing into sleep. The Motorola was in the other pocket too.

As Jimmy wiped his face on his sleeve, a new sound brought fresh terror. Those voices were coming closer! There was a thud of heavy feet along the corridor, then a creak as the bathroom door was tried. Jimmy' first reaction was to look around for a weapon. Nothing! Then he thought of the window. The door creaked again, then shook under the impact of a heavy kick. More croaking, then a heavier blow, as though someone was putting a shoulder to the door. The bolt held, but for how long? Already one screw was halfway out of its place.

Jimmy climbed up onto the john and began pulling again at the narrow window. It had opened about six inches before and Jimmy grasped it in a frenzy, pulling with all his might. It groaned open another couple of inches, still not enough. There was another heavy thud at the door and the tinkle of a screw falling to the tiles. Jimmy gave another almighty wrench, losing his footing as he did so. Slipping, he held on for dear life, the window shrieking as the rotten wood of the frame gave way, the whole thing coming with Jimmy as he fell.

He flung the window to one side, looking towards the blessed opening of cool night air. Without pause, Jimmy leapt onto the toilet again and pushed headfirst through the gap. With relief, he saw there was a narrow ledge running along this side of the building. With alarm, he heard the door behind him finally give way with a crash.

Belly scraping on the narrow frame, Jimmy wriggled frantically through the gap. The ledge was narrow but he got a hand to it and began sliding his legs out. One ankle was grabbed in a vice like grip and Jimmy kicked out in fear. There was a hissing cry as Jimmy's leg came free, minus his shoe. The movement tipped him out of the window and he barely managed to grasp the ledge below as his feet swung out into space. His other loafer came loose and clattered to the courtyard many feet below. Despite the situation, Jimmy swore at the loss of the expensive, hand-made shoes. Gritting his teeth, he scrabbled for some support with his feet and clasped the ledge firmly. His stockinged feet found the top of the window sill below and, for a second, he was able to draw breath.

His rest was interrupted by the appearance of head and shoulders through the window above. In the dark, under the shade of the hat, it was difficult to make out the man's features, apart from the slash of a twisted mouth and the bulbous, staring eyes. Grunting, the figure squirmed forward and reached down. Jimmy, thinking back to his old Judo days, didn't try and evade but reached up and curled his fingers into the lapel of the man's heavy coat. Then he abruptly bent his knees, pulling the man's weight out and over.

For a disquieting moment the man's face was inches from Jimmy. A waft of foul breath caused him to gag as the man opened his mouth impossibly wide, revealing small, serrated yellowed teeth. Jimmy thought the man was about to try and swallow his head whole, when the balance point tipped and his attacker flew over his shoulder. There was a dry croak of terror followed by a wet thud as the man hit the cobbles below.

Not daring to look over his shoulder Jimmy shuffled left. For a moment, he dangled in space until his feet found the top of the next window along. Glancing to his left he saw the slanted roof of a neighbouring building almost abutted up to the hotel at the end of the wall. Still not daring to look down, he repeated the manoeuvre twice more before swinging out and dropping down onto the grey slate roof. Above him, the head and shoulders of a second pursuer had appeared through the bathroom window. This one did not attempt to climb out but lifted his face to the clear, starlit sky and let out a series of loud, croaking moans interspersed with a weird clicking sound.

To Jimmy's horror, the cry was answered from some point in the distance, the noise echoing through the narrow streets. Jimmy made the peak of the roof and began to descend the opposite slope. Halfway down, his foot slipped on a patch of moss and he sat heavily, sliding towards the roof edge on his backside. Twisting, he managed to grab the gutter as he went over, wincing as the thin metal bit into his palms. Panting, he hung for a moment when, with a groan, the ancient guttering slowly gave way. Jimmy was half-lowered, half-fell to the sidewalk below, rolling as he hit the ground. He lay stunned for a moment, breathless, shoulder numb. Another barking cry brought him to a crouch. It was difficult to tell exactly where it came from, but judging it was from behind him, Jimmy began moving in the opposite direction.

The next few minutes were spent in a blind scrabble through narrow, empty lanes, that terrible croaking growing fainter as he fled. At length, Jimmy halted at the junction to wider street, Marsh Street according to the faded, green-streaked sign on the lamppost. Avoiding the pale glow of the street lamp, Jimmy turned right and made a crouched run, passing the dark windows of what looked to be abandoned houses.

A cool breeze from ahead carried the scent of sea; Jimmy reasoned he could maybe find and steal a boat and escape this madhouse. The dark entrance to an alleyway appeared ahead on the left and Jimmy darted into it. He risked a quick glance over his shoulder, the street behind remained quiet and empty. The far end of the alleyway opened out onto the sea front and Jimmy allowed himself a brief pause to draw breath. His shoulder was beginning to throb, his feet were sore and sweat stung his eyes. However the fresh ocean breeze helped revive him somewhat and, checking left and right, he crossed the open space to the low sea wall. Sliding over it, he dropped to the soft sand below and paused once more.

The coastline stretched away to each side. Not so much a beach as what looked like deposited sand, piled up between the breakwater and the shore. To his right, ruins of wharves jutted out from the shore to end in jagged, broken timbers. To the left, the coast curved round towards the harbour. Just beyond the mouth of the Manuxet River, Jimmy could just make out the vague outline of a few fishing boats visible in the clear night air. He was about to make for them when a sound caught his ear; that unholy croaking, clicking cry. Worse, it was echoed from more than one place, and as he watched, a group of figures burst onto the seafront, between him and the harbour. There looked to be around a dozen of them, some carrying lanterns or torches judging from the pinpricks of light.

Keeping low behind the wall, Jimmy turned and headed towards the wharves, hoping he would leave no footprints in the sand. Within minutes, he made the ruins, moving into the shadows beneath the crumbling wooden structures. His pursuers were now out of sight but Jimmy started as he heard more noise from closer by. He drew further into shade as another group of around five slouched figures appeared above the sea wall. One leant over and shone a torch back and forth along the sand before the group began moving south, towards the wharves.

Jimmy picked his way across fallen timbers, now completely under the wharf buildings, the cold sea lapping at his ankles. Above, he saw an opening in the floor and, scrambling up a worm-eaten beam, he climbed into one of the old buildings. The place creaked alarmingly as Jimmy moved gingerly through the interior. Holes in the roof and walls let in just enough light for Jimmy to avoid the few old barrels and crates that still remained. Aside from the creaks, the only other sounds were the hiss of the sea and the soft whisper of the breeze.

Moving through a door, which he shut softly behind him, Jimmy found he had gone as far as he could. Half of the room he now stood in had fallen away into the sea. He lay on his belly and slid to the jagged edge of the floor. About fifteen feet below him dark waters swirled. A flash of light caught his eye, ahead, out at sea. There it was again. Straining his eyes Jimmy could make out a darker line against the shifting waves, way out past the harbour. It was from there that the flash emanated; light green, he thought, though with a curious purple tinge.

Jimmy was no maritime expert but he had been around enough yachts and marinas to know that this was no navigation light; it looked more like a bonfire or live flame. But out at sea? That was insane! He glanced back round at the shore behind him, drawing breath in with a start at an answering flash from inland. This was a more conventional red light, stuttering in some unknown sequence. It was fairly high up and looked to be coming from some tower, perhaps one of the cupolas he had seen on the larger houses on his earlier drive around town.

Jimmy struggled to rationalise the situation. Since leaving the cafe, very little had made sense. He could handle his drink with the best of them, why would a slug of rum leave him so smashed? And why were these people chasing him? The guys in the hotel he could maybe understand, if it was plain and simple robbery. But the rest of the town? He'd come to the town with nothing but good intentions and, as far as he knew, had not upset or offended anyone. He'd met the Mayor, for Christ's sake! Yet his car tyres had been slashed, three heavies tried to break into his room and now he was being chased by what looked like an angry lynch mob.

Hoping against hope, Jimmy took the Motorola out of his pocket and tried another call. *Shit, still no signal.* He put the phone away and found himself beginning to shiver. Delayed shock, he figured. Crawling back from the edge, he backed into the remaining corner of the room and put his head in his hands.

How long he sat like this, he didn't know. It was a heavy, rhythmic creaking and slithering that brought him back to the present. Someone... something... was approaching the door. Jimmy huddled tighter into the corner as the steps grew nearer. There was a tense pause then the door creaked, slowly swinging inwards. The foul, fishy odour grew stronger. Jimmy was shielded by the door but had the impression of some terrible thing behind it, the same feeling as earlier in the hotel.

The door was now agape but the opener did not enter the ruined room. Jimmy stared aghast at what appeared around the edge of the door. Fingers, clutching the rotting wood; though at first he thought they were worms, or large maggots. Plump and white, they glistened in the pale moonlight. Independently they wriggled, with a curiously boneless motion. With a further start Jimmy noted that each finger, if that is what they were, tapered to a point. Jimmy bit on his fist to stop himself from crying out; he fancied he could hear a soft, wheezing hiss. Then that strange, alien hand was retracted, closing the door with it. The slithering started again, moving away and Jimmy allowed a small sob to escape his lips.

He reasoned he had two choices; stay in place and eventually be discovered or move and at least have some chance of escape. But where to go? Any movement along the sea front would likely be spotted. He wracked his brains trying to visualise the notes and map. He knew that the town was edged by marsh on at least one side. Perhaps he could flee into the marsh and hide there or, better still, work his way back up to a main road. Having a plan did something to restore Jimmy's nerve and he stood and listened at the door for a few minutes. Hearing nothing, he opened the door and began retracing his steps through the rotting superstructure.

Minutes later, he was again crouched by the sea wall, swivelling a nervous gaze left and right. Both lights were still flashing back and forth but the nearby streets seemed clear.

Thinking he was nearer to the south edge of town than the north, Jimmy slipped over the wall and plunged into the dark lane beyond, moving swiftly through the narrow streets once more, heading, as much as he could, away from the hotel square and that distant, flashing light. The houses here were just as desolate, in fact some had tumbled completely into ruin.

Jimmy moved past them in a stumbling run, occasionally glancing back over his shoulder for signs of pursuit. At the flicker of light behind him, Jimmy ducked into one of the ruins. The door lay amidst the weeds and the windows sagged empty and open. From his vantage point he saw a small group cross the street some fifty feet back the way he had came. They looked to have no clue as to where he was and Jimmy made to move out. A scuttling sound froze him to the spot.

Over the edge of one of the windows appeared two spindly, chitinous legs. They tapped around for a second before being joined by another two, which then heaved a nightmare bulk into view. The thing was the size of a small dog. Several long, multi-jointed legs sprouted from a round, oval body. It looked to be covered in a thick shell, dotted with patches of green sea moss. Worst of all was the thing's face; despite the crab-like body, it had a small, pinched, quasi-human face at the front of the shell. At least he could make out a pair of solid, jet eyes, and a small nose-like protuberance set atop a pair of wickedly curved pincers.

The thing reared up at the sight of Jimmy and the pincers opened, revealing a sphincter-like opening that pulsed, emitting a high-pitched shriek that echoed and rebounded along the narrow lane. With a moan of horror, Jimmy hurled himself back out into the street. The thing remained shrieking, legs wildly twitching and its call was answered. The group hove back into view and Jimmy decided the time for stealth was gone. He put his head down and ran.

His appearance brought an awful wailing howl from the group behind him and he heard the slap of feet as they gave pursuit. To his relief he saw the street ended ahead in a weed-covered vacant lot. Ignoring the sting of nettles and the grasp of brambles he plunged into it. The clamour behind him grew, he guessed perhaps another group had joined in the chase.

Beating his way through the lot, Jimmy burst out into a small patch of open land. He never thought he would be so pleased to have the stink of marsh in his nostrils. Despite the noise behind him, Jimmy took a moment to think. Plunging blindly ahead was asking for trouble; plus it would be the expected thing to do. Instead, Jimmy turned and moved to his right, running in a crouch along the dirt track that ran along the southern perimeter of the town. A hundred yards along he found a heap of timbers, what looked like the collapsed ruins of some kind of shed. Kneeling, he moved some of the wood to make a space, then crawled into the small gap, pulling the timber back over him.

Through a narrow gap he had a view of the track. Sweat trickled down his back as he shifted slightly against a piece of wood jabbing into his thigh, then froze as a group of figures shuffled into view. Most of them were those he had seen before; slouched figures in heavy coats, limping, heads slowly turning back and forth in search of their prey. Leading them, swinging an old fashioned lantern before her, strode Sonia, her face set in furious concentration. That was the first shock.

The second and bigger shock was the nature of two figures that followed the group. Man-like in shape and general outline, there was nothing human about the way they moved; a curious hopping, slithering motion, as though this were not their natural environment. Scaly and shiny, their naked bellies shining white in the moonlight, they barked and croaked, as if ordering the rest of the group. Their heads were the worse; fish-like, unblinking eyes, thin-lipped wide mouths. Gill-like slits at the neck pulsed open and closed and the reality of the source of the Innsmouth look finally crashed full into Jimmy's consciousness. The awareness, along with the weight of the night's events overwhelmed him and Jimmy fell into blessed oblivion.

He awoke some time later, the pale promise of dawn in the air. Stirring slowly, he glanced around before removing himself from the hiding place. The air was cold and damp and he pulled his tattered and stained jacket tightly around his shivering frame. With a last glimpse at the hell-town of Innsmouth, he turned and set off into the marsh. It was a couple of hours later that he found a main road and another hour's walk along it brought him to a service station. He burst into the forecourt store, much to the surprise of the young man behind the counter, who recoiled at the mud-stained, tattered apparition before him.

The newcomer grabbed a can of coke from the cooler,

threw down a ten dollar bill from his wallet, popped the tab and downed the drink in one. Then, panting, he steadied himself with a hand on the counter, before seeming to come to and realising where he was.

"Sorry," he said. "I broke down further up the road. Had to trek across the marsh. I've had a hell of a night." The man then reached into his pocket, causing the youth to flinch again.

"Shit. My phone. I must have dropped it in the marsh. Do you have a phone I could use?"

The youth nodded and pointed to the public pay phone on the far wall, giving the man some coins in his change for the drink. Despite the man's appearance, the attendant could see he was wearing an expensive suit, and he caught the flash of a Rolex at the man's wrist. Maybe his story was true? In any event, the man moved to the phone and made a call.

Jimmy' first call was to home. It went to answer phone. The second call was to Peter Hawkins' cell phone, it was picked up before the second ring.

"Peter...it's Jimmy... Jimmy O'Brien."

The older man's voice was loud in the earpiece. "Jimmy, where the hell are you? We're out of our mind with worry!"

"I'm just outside Innsmouth. On the Arkham road, a service station." Jimmy' voice cracked.

"Okay, don't worry Jimmy, I'm on the way. You can tell me all about it when I'm there."

"Jackie, I rang her, there was no answer."

"It's alright, Jackie is with us. She phoned last night when you didn't come home. Kiri went to pick her up, we'll bring her with us. You just hold tight, feller, help is on the way."

Jimmy burbled his thanks before staggering back outside,

leaving the receiver hanging on the cable.

Hawkins' Isuzu Trooper swept into the station forecourt and before it had come to a halt, Jackie was out of the door and running towards Jimmy, sat with his back to the warming brickwork. Soundlessly he rose and the pair hugged tightly. Jackie, eyes tearing up, laughed.

"You stink, mister. Let's get you home for a bath." Jimmy nodded. He was about to tell his wife about the creatures he had seen when two more figures burst from the vehicle.

"Daddy! Daddy!" The children flew into his arms and now it was Jimmy who broke down into tears.

Oblivious to this, Lauren piped up "Daddy you are very smelly! Pooh!" The remark brought laughter, not only from Jimmy but also from Hawkins who now patted Jimmy on the shoulder.

"Come on, young man. Let's get you where you need to be." He ushered Jimmy into the backseat of the SUV with the rest of his family. Kiri turned and smiled from the front seat.

"Everyone aboard? Then let's go!" said Hawkins. He put the Trooper into reverse in preparation to leave the forecourt. Kiri had produced a flask and some cups. "Now who would like some hot chocolate?" she asked. The kids both squealed "Meeee!"

Jimmy gratefully accepted the plastic mug and sipped, starting to relax. He rested his head against the leather interior and glanced across at Jackie and the kids, also settling into the comfortable seats. *It had been a long night for all of them*, Jimmy thought. He closed his eyes, happy to be safe and warm.

A jolt as the SUV hit a pothole brought him out of his doze. Something he'd glimpsed out of the window confused him. A sign, faded and green with algae; it said Innsmouth. He tried to say something but found himself unable to move. An inarticulate groan escaped his lips and drool ran down his chin. Kiri turned and fixed him with a piercing glare. She nudged her husband.

"Still awake?" Hawkins glanced at him in the rear view mirror. "My word, you are a resistant one aren't you? Sonia was right."

Jimmy struggled against the fog that filled his brain and the lead that filled his limbs. He saw they were driving through the streets of Innsmouth. Hawkins continued.

"You see, as Mayor Marsh may have mentioned, Innsmouth is in desperate need of fresh blood but there just aren't any visitors these days. The new development will bring plenty of tourists, no one will notice if a few go missing now and then. Of course, we have to convince the Elders of that. They don't really understand the modern world. And sacrifices have to be made"

Jimmy managed to stammer, "S-sacrifices?"

"Yes, dear," replied Kiri. "It's a tradition, you see. These out of the way places are very set in their ways. In fact, their old ways came from my people; old Obed Marsh brought them over. You'll meet him later. I'm afraid it won't be a pleasant meeting for you, but sacrifices need to be made."

Her husband explained. "Field was fine but he wasn't my choice. No family, you see. Still, his coming here paved the way, you might say. The Elders saw that we were serious, that we were prepared to commit ourselves fully to the Order."

"Please..." mumbled Jimmy. "Take me. Don't hurt the children."

Kiri smiled and glanced at the sleeping kids. "Hurt the children? Why on Earth would we do that? They are very precious to us! Don't worry Jimmy, your children will be very well cared for. After all, they are the future of Innsmouth."

By now, the vehicle had reached the circular green and drew to a halt outside the large, Masonic building.

"The Esoteric Order of Dagon," sighed Hawkins dreamily. He turned to Jimmy. "Not many outsiders get to see the inside of this place, let alone take part in a ritual. You and your wife should consider yourselves honoured. Shall we go in, honey?"

The pair disembarked, Kiri fetching a pair of dark red robes from the trunk. The rear doors opened and strong, sinuous limbs gently lifted Jimmy and Jackie from their seats. Barely able to even move his head, Jimmy glanced up the steps to see a twisted, robed figure standing patiently in the shadow of the portico. He managed one shallow, hoarse scream before being carried inside.

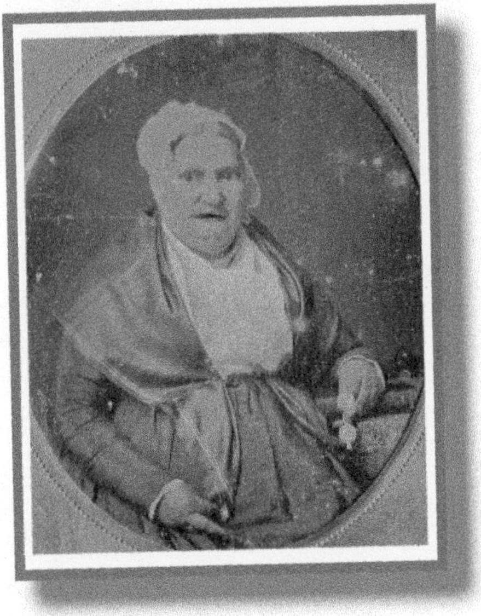

THE WATCHER

Sometimes, when I sit and think
I have to remind myself to blink.
For sitting quiet, as I dare,
An observer may notice my glassy stare.
Then, attention drawn, wonder apace
At the ghostly pallor of my face,
The fleshy lips which, when peeled,
Sharp, serrated teeth reveal.
And should they shoulder grab or clasp,
Might at my bonelessness remark.
If I perchance grabbed straying wrist
T'would reveal the strength of my flabby fist.
Then forced to flee into the street
I may be, mission incomplete.
For far ahead of shoal I've swam
To reconnoitre the ways of man,
Reporting back into the deeps
Where in the darkness, deathless, sleeps
Our Dread Lord who none dare name
For fear they may His attention gain.
But when the stars roll in the skies
Shall once again our Dread Lord rise.
And crashing like a wave roll o'er
This human world and, in time, restore
The natural order as once it stood...
Where Deep Ones rule... and man is food.

INNSMOUTH ECHOES

URBEX

Jon flicked back his floppy blonde fringe and refolded the Ordnance Survey map as best he could in the confined space of the driver's seat. He turned to his friend in the back seat of the Golf gti, pointing to a spot on the map.

"We've just come through Long Sutton so I reckon we must be about here. I'm sure that was a sign for Lutton we just passed."

His passenger Iain, also in his early twenties, though prematurely balding, waved his mobile in the air and scowled into his beard.

"I'm getting no signal, so I can't help." He turned to his girlfriend sat next to him. "Tabbs, what does it say in the book?"

She brushed her multi-coloured dreads away from her face and peered at the book in front of her again.

"It says here through Long Sutton, head north to Lutton -"

"And then left at Mutton, over the bridge to Button?" piped up Gem, the front seat passenger. Dark haired and studious, she sighed and sank back into her black puffer jacket.

"I'm freezing and need a wee. Can we stop at a cafe somewhere?"

Jon shook his head and turned the heating up. Then making

a decision, he indicated and pulled out of the small lay-bay, back onto the narrow country lane heading north. His decision was rewarded when within ten minutes, they drove into the main street of Lutton. Even better, there was pub on the High Street, the Jolly Crispin. Jon pulled into the car park and the four young friends made their way into the warm interior of the pub.

It was a Wednesday lunchtime, the place was not that busy but every head turned at the appearance of newcomers. Tabbs was used to it; a nose stud, colourful dreads and assorted beads and bangles tended to draw attention anywhere outside of cosmopolitan Cambridge. Iain, stocky and surly, could look intimidating with his tribal tats and eyebrow piercing, a look he utilised to full effect now, returning the stares of the locals as they made their way to the bar. Jon, oblivious and ever cheerful, smiled at the landlady, ordered a round of drinks and asked for the lunch menu. The landlady returned his smile and, in motherly fashion, said, "Take a table over there, ducks, I'll bring the drinks and menu over."

The four friends sat and the locals returned to their conversations or newspapers. Jon got out the OS map again and, as the drinks arrived, began running his finger over it.

"We can't be far off. The place is supposed to be not far from the coast. You can't go much further east from here without getting your feet wet."

The landlady peered over his shoulder. "Are you lost, loves? Where are you heading?"

Gem peered over her specs and said "Neatisham. There's an old MOD place there."

The landlady's face fell. She hurriedly gave out the rest of the drinks.

"Don't know what you'd want to go there for. Empty old place, that's all that is." She hurried off back to the sanctuary of her bar.

"Old and empty is exactly why we want to go," chuckled Jon.

He was the driving force behind this little band of Urbexers. That's what they liked to call themselves. Urban exploration, it had become quite the thing over the last few years. Small groups of intrepid Urbexers gaining covert access to old buildings. Deserted hospitals, old army bases, they'd even gone into closed-down tube stations beneath the streets of London. They went in purely to have a look around and take photos, which were then shared on various websites and forums.

Others of their kind took pride in scaling high towers or buildings, filming themselves perched on ledges or hanging off gantries. But for this Urbex group it was enough to get unnoticed into a place, have a nose around, get some snaps, then sneak back out, leaving everything as they found it. *Take only photos, leave only footprints* was their motto.

Jon had come across the story of Neatisham while researching old airfields in the area. They had already been into RAF Upwood further to the west, a rambling collection of decaying buildings. Neatisham promised something more enticing; as part of the RAF's Cold War defence system, it housed a secret control and command bunker. According to the info, the place comprised a radar station set inside a compound, beneath which lay a comprehensive underground bunker system. The RAF had vacated in the early 60s, though the place had remained in use by the military until it was damaged by a fire in the late 80s. Since then, it had remained empty, like so many relics of the Cold War that lay scattered along the East Coast. Despite having been decommissioned over twenty years ago, the site was steeped in mystery with very little detailed information available. When researching, Jon had discovered that when the relevant files were released to the Public Records Office in the 90s, many were missing. He even spoke to an RAF archivist, who told him that although boxes containing thousands of photographs had been rehoused in new storage facilities, no pictures relating to RAF Neatisham could be found. Furthermore, it seemed that all the relevant indexes had been destroyed.

This kind of mystery was meat and drink to the Urbexers who thrived on tales of dark deeds and local lore and legend. So they'd set aside a couple of days to locate and explore this place, fully equipped with Go-Pros, night vision cameras and other assorted tools of the trade.

The food came over shortly after the drink, delivered by the now wordless landlady. Suitably refreshed the group returned to the car and began their search again. It was late afternoon when they finally found the turning. They had missed it on the first two passes, it being an old farm gate largely obscured by undergrowth. The October sun hung low in the sky, colouring the air a soft orange. An arrowhead of geese honked overhead as Iain opened the squeakily protesting gate. Beyond lay a simple track leading across the edge of a flat field.

The car swayed as Jon took it down the track, which led them to a chainlink fence. Excitedly they got out of the car, to stand staring at their prize through the rusting mesh. In the centre of a small clearing, on an island of tarmac amongst the long grass and weeds stood, what to all intents and purposes, looked like a 50s chalet style bungalow. Its doors and windows were closed with heavy, white metal shutters. Weeds pushed up through the tarmac, the grey roof was half covered with a thick moss. The air was hushed and still.

"Boom!" smiled Jon. Moving along the fence he came to a gate, secured with a large, rusting padlock. He rattled the lock to no effect. Bolt croppers were an option but the group preferred not to cause damage if they could help it.

"Over here!" called Tabbs. She crouched by a section of the wire fence that looked to have been torn away from its supporting post. The chain link had been pushed outwards and Tabbs easily lifted it, making a hole big enough for someone to crawl through. Jon was about to suggest getting the gear from the car, when a noise stopped him. They could hear a tractor approaching along the edge of the field, out of sight but growing louder. Without a word, the group jumped back in the car, Jon reversing as fast as he dared go back down the track. Ahead, they could see the roof of the tractor over the hedge and watched as it reached the edge of the field, before swinging back round for a return trip.

"Shit, looks like he'll be there for a while." Iain said.

"No probs," replied Jon. "We know where it is now, let's give it an hour or so, come back after dark. He'll be gone by then."

Plan agreed, Jon revved the engine and reversed back out onto the main road. There was a sickening thump as he did so; the four friends looked at each other before jumping out of the car.

"Oh my god...." Gem put a hand to her mouth and turned away. Iain took a closer look.

"You've hit a badger, mate. "

Jon moved round to the rear of car, grimacing at the black and white corpse that lay under his rear bumper. Blood poured from the creature's nose and it was quite clearly dead.

"Shit, shit, shit," Jon hissed. "Give me a hand Iain. Let's move it onto the verge."

"I ain't touching it!" Iain raised his hands.

"Oh, for fuck's sake!" Tabbs bent and, with some tenderness, lifted the heavy animal and laid it to rest on the grass verge.

"You know those things carry fleas," warned Gem, backing away from Tabbs.

"Well, it was a quick death," shrugged Jon, "And look on the bright side, we can use it as a marker for the entrance."

Iain grinned. "Perhaps I should take it's skull?"

"You wouldn't even pick it up," mumbled Tabbs as they returned to the car. Badger removed, Jon three point turned and they drove back towards the pub.

"Didn't find it, then?" asked the landlady.

"Nope," said Jon. "Reckon we'll have a couple of drinks then head back home."

Mollified, the landlady poured the drinks and the group retired to the same table they'd used at lunchtime. The pub began filling with evening trade, local farmers from the look of it. Jon nudged the group as he overhead one newcomer talking at the bar.

"Saw a car up on the old bunker track." The man was telling

his neighbouring drinker.

His companion took a sip of stout and replied. "Kids, was it? Looking for somewhere for a quick cuddle?"

"They'll get more than a cuddle up there." the first man responded. "I won't even keep sheep in that field since... well, since that lass went missing."

Jon was torn between asking for more information and keeping a low profile. In the end, curiosity won out.

"Who went missing up there, then?" he called across to the farmer.

The man pivoted on his barstool and ran a steely gaze over the group. "Young lass from the village. Five year back. Only eight she were. Went off for a walk across the fields one teatime and never came home. As though she disappeared into thin air."

Iain was about to make a witty retort when Jon kicked him under the table.

"That's awful!" he replied. "What did the police say?"

"Them's didn't say much at all. Had a look round, found nothing. Some other types came down a couple of weeks later, suits. Asked a lot of questions and then fitted new shutters to the place."

"Is that where she went missing, then? "asked Gem

"Don't know but she was last seen on the edge of that field. Place ain't right, mark my words." With that, the man slid off his stool and carried his pint to the fruit machine, which he began feeding pound coins.

"Mystery upon mystery!" mused Iain.

Gem shivered. "I don't like it. Perhaps we shouldn't go back there?"

Iain grinned and began making a low clucking sound, growing louder as he flailed his arms.

"Stop being a dick, Iain" Tabbs scolded. "Gem has a point."

Jon finished his pint and thudded the empty glass onto the beer mat. "Oh, come on! We're here now. And when have we ever let a few local scary stories put us off? It's probably a wind up anyway. I bet they want to keep people way cos they use it for dogging!"

That broke the tension and the group filed out of the pub. A kebab van had just set up shop in the car park, much to Iain's delight. He insisted on "kebabs before 'sploring". They ate in the car, Jon none too keen about the stink of onions and the potential for sauce spillage on his upholstery. Once done, they were soon driving back along the lane looking for the entrance.

"I swear it was along here but I can't see the badger!" Jon complained. He pulled the car over and got out.

"Yep, this is it, there's the gate." He swept his torch along the grass verge. "But where's the badger?"

"I guess it wasn't dead," said Gem out of the open window. "Perhaps you just stunned it?"

"This badger is not dead," piped up Iain in a Pythonesque voice., "It is merely stunned!"

Jon opened the gate again and, headlights off, drove carefully down the track. The four were soon gathered round the rip in the fence. Jon went through first, taking equipment filled rucksacks as they were pushed through to him. The others followed and they approached the squat building. A gibbous moon was beginning to show above the trees, the shutters shone like bone in its light. Light evening dew soaked the hems of their trousers as they moved though overgrown weeds and long grass to the side of the bungalow. Gem jumped as an owl hooted nearby. Iain sniggered, earning him a slap on the shoulder from Tabbs.

"Ssshh!" whispered Jon. "Look, the shuttering is loose." Sure enough, although the shutter on the corner window looked firm, it had swung open to Jon's touch. Darkness yawned beyond. Jon turned and grinned, face pale in the black hoody.

"In we go!"

He switched on his head torch on and climbed smoothly over the sill, Gem and Iain followed. A strange urge made Tabbs take one last look round. The field and track appeared empty, the Autumn moon bathing the scene in a soft glow. With a prickling feeling at the back of her neck, she hoisted a leg over the sill and stepped into the gloom.

The interior was as bare and derelict as the outside. There was no pretence of domesticity, just a single large, blank room taking up the whole floor space. Torch beams revealed a concrete floor and a heap of rags in the corner. Gem held a hand to her face.

"Eeuurgh, what is that smell!"

Even Iain had to agree, the place smelled rank. A potent combination of mould and rotting fish. They moved around, the smell was worse over by the rags.

"Here, this must be the entrance." Tabbs had found what looked like the door to a broom cupboard in the corner. It swung open easily, revealing a set of iron rungs set into brickwork, leading into the depths below.

"Now we're talking, "smiled Jon, moving across to the ladder. Head torch in place, rucksack on back, he began the descent into darkness. He soon found himself in a white-walled corridor that stretched off in both directions. Moving left, as the others descended, he came to a heavy closed door at the end of the passageway, AUTHORISED PERSONNEL ONLY stencilled in large red letters across it.

Jon grasped the lever and pulled. The door swung open easily enough, inside looked like some kind of generator room, complete with DANGER:HIGH VOLTAGE signs. Jon quickly found the master switch and, holding his breath and crossing his fingers, flipped it down. His prayers were answered as a low hum filled the room and the fluorescent lighting overhead flickered into life. Iain's grinning face appeared round the door.

"You found the on switch, then?"

"Yep," Jon replied. "One good thing about these old places, their power systems were built to last."

In the corridor Tabbs was already taking photos as Gem clambered down the ladder.

"Well at least the smell is better down here," she said, shifting her rucksack. The corridor stretched ahead, bare except for the overhead trunking, lit only by the dim glow of bulkhead lights. Thirty paces on, the corridor dog-legged to the right and the group found themselves standing before a huge, red metal door. It stood ajar and they passed through into an antechamber. Opposite stood an identical door, also ajar.

"Nice of them to leave the place open," muttered Iain.

"Perhaps they left in a rush," responded Tabbs. "Wasn't there a fire here in the 80s?"

"There was," Jon confirmed. "Though you'd have thought the place would've been secured after that. Still, makes our job easier!"

The group pushed on into a strange chamber. It wasn't much

wider than the corridor, one wall filled with small, circular protuberances.

"What are they?" asked Gem. Iain touched one of the devices.

"It's a blast valve room. A nuke going off upstairs would produce high speed winds, up to a thousand miles an hour. These valves were designed to reduce the pressure."

"Be a hell of an ear-pop otherwise," smiled Jon, fishing for his camera in his rucksack. One more steel door lay beyond, with an attendant RESTRICTED AREA sign. A guard booth and turnstile had been built into the entrance way. It had a small counter opening, like in a Post Office, upon which another sign read PLEASE RING AND WAIT. Before anyone could stop him, Iain leaned forward and pressed the button. They heard the distant ring of a bell and the lights flickered overhead. For a brief second they were in total darkness.

Iain laughed at their expressions and said, "Well, we rang and waited, no one came. Shall we go in?"

Without waiting for a reply he pushed through the turnstile. The rest followed, snapping pictures as they went. Gem was the last one out of the valve room. Before she left, she thought she heard a sound back behind her. A distant echo, perhaps, of a steel shutter being pulled back into place? Putting it down to nerves, she shook her head and followed the others.

The bunker was huge and the group was soon immersed in a warren of tunnels, living quarters and machinery rooms. The electrics seemed to be working okay in most places, though odd areas either flickered or remained dark. Smoke marks and fire damage became more evident the deeper they went, increasing until they reached the Control Room.

It looked as though this large space had been the epicentre of the fire. Banks of old fashioned computers and control panels lined the walls, there was a huge scorch mark in the middle of the floor. Files and folders lay strewn around, the smell of burnt paper still hung in the air; plastic chairs had melted into Dali-esque shapes. The far end of the room lay in darkness, only two lights by the door were working. Jon flicked on his head torch and jumped.

"Wassup?" asked Iain, as he riffled through a singed folder.

"I thought I saw something move over there." Jon laughed nervously.

"Well, let's go take a look!" Iain dropped the folder, switched on his own torch and moved to the far end of the room.

"There's another doorway here." He went through it. "And another corridor leading off it - "

At once a high-pitched scream filled the room, each of the three friends jumped with fright. Tabbs was the first to recover, racing to the darkened doorway through which Iain had disappeared. Her fingers trembled as she flicked on her hand-held torch, shining it through the door to reveal the laughing face of Iain in its pallid glow. Bent double, sides heaving, he clutched the wall for support as the rest of the group came through the doorway.

"Your faces," he gasped for breath.

"Fuck's sake!" hissed Tabbs. She was about to chastise Iain further when a sound brought them all up short. An echoing clang behind them. This time there could be no mistake, it was a heavy door closing.

"Shit, you think someone saw us coming in?" asked Gem. "Perhaps it's the police?"

"Well, if it is, they have to find us to kick us out!" said Jon defiantly. "Let's push on down this corridor. But keep the noise down! And no more arsing around, Iain!"

The group followed the corridor along, then down some steps into a lower level. The smell from bungalow was present here again, not quite so strong but definitely in the air. This level looked to be made up of staff quarters. They moved through a large canteen and into a kitchen. All the cupboard doors were open and empty boxes and food cartons lay scattered about the place. Two larder rooms off to the side looked similarly ransacked.

They moved back through to the canteen, finding that the next door along the corridor led into a dormitory. No lights were working here, but by torchlight they took in the name tabs, the clothes that hung in open lockers, the beds that looked as though sleepers had just risen from them. There were even mugs of tea on bedside tables; at least, that's what they imagined lay beneath the mould. A few peeling posters were tacked to the wall. The group were hushed.

"It's like they just left," breathed Gem.

"This dates it though," Jon smiled, pointing to the poster of a woman tennis player scratching her bare backside displayed over one bed.

"Seventies, right?" asked Tabbs, scowling at Iain bounding over to take a closer look.

"Puts it into perspective that people were actually living down here," said Jon.

"Did they have kids down here, too?" asked Gem from a corner of the room.

"What makes you ask that?" replied Jon.

"These... look, I just found them by this bed."

The group gathered round the bed in question, that rotting

smell in evidence again. Gem lifted her hands to reveal a pair of shoes. Small shoes, a child's shoes. The kind a young girl might wear.

Jon swallowed hard. "I don't think they would have had kids down here."

"Maybe for an drill or exercise?" offered Tabbs.

"Yep, maybe." Jon replied doubtfully. "In any case, there's no one here now. I think we've seen enough, how about heading back up top?"

"Guys... look at this!" Iain had wandered over to the far side of the dorm and was playing his torch across the end wall. The group moved to stand behind him.

"Fuck! What is that?" Tabbs whispered. Iain's torch showed a strange mural scrawled across the magnolia paintwork. Crude figures, almost stick-like, as though drawn by a child. Some looked military, wearing caps and uniforms. Others were misshapen, with claw like hands. Moving across, they saw what was clearly a depiction of a fire or flames, orange, yellow and red.

Then nothing more, except for the startling depiction of a face and some words. The face was a distorted version of a human one, like a reflection from a funfair mirror. The eyes bulged, the skull looked deformed, the jaw receded. The mouth was open, showing pointed, shark-like teeth. Next to it, in a rough scrawl, were two words.

IT HURTS.

The group looked at the childish drawings and then at each other. It was Gem who spotted the crayons on the floor, worn down or broken in two.

"Well, this must've been a kid," said Iain.

"No," Jon replied. "Look how high they are. There's nothing here to stand on, a kid couldn't reach that high."

Gem let out a sob of fear. "I want to get out of here."

Jon nodded. "Yeah, me too. Let's head back the way we came. If that is Old Bill up there we can tell them about this. Whatever this is."

As one, they moved back to the corridor outside the dorm. They played their torches around nervously, now, imagining some grim shape lurking in the shadows. Even Iain was subdued, hesitating in thought as the group moved on ahead of him. He was about to express the thought when he felt something grab his rucksack and pull him sharply backwards. Before he could cry out, a foul-smelling, slimy hand was clamped across his nose and mouth. His last impressions were of a foul odour and the crazy strobing of his head torch on the corridor ceiling.

The group had moved along the corridor to just past the canteen room. It was Gem who noticed Iain's absence.

"Shit," murmured Jon. "If he's dicking about again..."

The two girls followed as Jon stormed back along the corridor, swearing under his breath.

"Iain! Iain!" he called out in a hoarse whisper. There was a sound and movement ahead, from within an open doorway. Tabbs moved forward and shone her torch full onto a scene of horror. Iain lay on the floor, head tilted back, eyes glassy and unseeing. Above him crouched a hideous shape. It glistened in the torch light, its skin mottled grey and green. Vaguely man-shape, yet its features were distinctly batrachians; bulbous, unblinking eyes stared at them from under a misshapen brow. The stench of sea rot and death rolled from it in waves. Like some obscene, antediluvian idol it squatted there.

Iain's torso lay ripped open and, as they watched, the thing inserted a hand into the bloody hole and pulled out a dripping, red gobbet, which it crammed into its slit-like mouth, swallowing with a shiver of delight. Jon's mind struggled to make sense of the scene; an image of the earlier kebab flashed, unbidden, into his mind and he reeled away, vomiting as he turned. Gem screamed and dropped to her knees, hands covering her eyes. Tabbs reeled back into the wall, torch dropping from nerveless fingers, plunging the terrible vision back into darkness.

Jon turned back, shining his head torch into the doorway but the thing had gone. Iain's torn and bloody corpse still remained.

"Fuckfuckfuck…" Jon was gibbering. Gem remained kneeling. Tabb swallowed hard and took control; she clutched Jon by the shoulder and slapped him hard.

"Come on! We've got to get out of here!" she snapped.

Jon took a deep breath and composed himself. "Yes, yes. Grab Gem, let's run for it."

Gem was quietly sobbing but allowed herself to be stood up and led. The three ran as fast as they dared, to the junction at the end of the corridor, then along and down some steps, to be confronted by another heavy door that lay slightly ajar..

"Shit, this isn't right. We didn't come this way before." Tabbs cried.

Jon glanced around quickly. "Quick, through here, get that door shut behind us."

They pushed through, slamming the thick door behind them. Inside was what looked like a small reception area. Tabbs moved quickly to the desk.

" Help me shift this against the door."

The pair pushed and pulled until the door was barricaded. Gem, meanwhile, had wandered, in a daze, along the small corridor that led from the room. The pair found her slumped in a corner, sobbing. Tabbs did her best to comfort her while Jon looked around, exploring the various doors that opened off of the corridor.

"Come and see this!" he called.

Tabbs guided Gem into a small office. The desk against the far wall was overflowing with folders and papers. Jon had been sifting through them and held up what looked like a journal or diary.

"What is all this stuff?" asked Tabbs.

"I don't know." Jon indicated the desk. "Most of these look like official papers. But this," he brandished the journal. "It looks like a personal account from one of the staff here. See, it's in the flyleaf." He read from the page."LAC Stephen Manning, RAF Neatisham. First entry is May 15th 1984."

Tabbs, meanwhile had been scanning the folders on the desk.

"This is mental." She flicked through some more papers, then read out loud.

"Operation Tide. Top Secret. Aims: to establish meaningful contact with agencies dwelling on or near the East Angllain coastline. To ascertain true background and ancestry of "amphibian hybrids" (see shared US Intelligence reports *Operation Ashdod* 1928, *Yankton State Mental Hospital Reports* 1928-49, *Ahnenerbe Projekt Leo report*, 1945.)

Purpose: potential recruitment of AH for intelligence / military purpose. Further insight into potential occult, social and political ramifications of entities known as *Great Old Ones*."

"Manning backs it up." Jon had been scanning the journal, lighting the pages with his head torch. He read out.

"Got a quick glimpse of top secret papers while filing. Occult? Military? Why would they believe in such nonsense?"

He flicked on several pages. "Here we go. This is from September 85. Rumours of a sub-section and external tunnels confirmed. Managed to slip through security during the last attack exercise. There's a warren down there! From the smell they must extend all the way to the coast."

Jon flicked ahead a few pages and read some more. "Carpeted by CO. Seems I was caught on CCTV entering restricted area. He didn't seem concerned though, in fact he laughed and told me I'd find out "soon enough." What does that mean?"

Tabbs meanwhile, had found another folder containing some old black and white photos. She passed them to Jon. The figures in the pictures were fuzzy and blurred but bore resemblance to the thing that had killed Iain.

"These photos look to be decades old," murmured Gem. Jon continued from the diary.

"Dear God, it's all true. And the worst of it is, now I know why I was chosen for this posting. It's all down to ancestry. I have the heritage, it seems, and they want to change me!" He leafed on a couple more pages, then nodded. "This has to stop. Last night they showed me photographs and films of those things. Awful. This is not right. No point going through the channels, have to take direct action. For all our sakes."

Tabbs looked over his shoulder. "January 18th 1986." She

thought for a second and then scrabbled through the papers, muttering, "I saw it here earlier... that date....ah, here!" She held a yellowed newspaper in her hand and waved it triumphantly.

"Here," she cried, "the headline story! January 20th, fire at RAF station." Jon moved to shine the torch fully on the page as Tabbs read out.

"Local fire crews were called to an emergency at Neatisham in the early hours of the morning. Initial reports indicate a major fire at an RAF facility just outside the village of Lutton. Two fire crew are reported dead and one in hospital. No further casualties are known as yet."

Jon shuffled again through the pile on the desk. "Here's another report, a few days later." He scanned through the first couple of paragraphs, then read, "Investigators report the blaze was started deliberately. The arsonist has been named as Stephen Manning, a Lowestoft man, who had been serving at the facility for some months. The MOD reports that Manning was killed in the blaze that he started. His motives are unknown."

They sat silent for a moment, attempting to make a coherent picture from these fragmentary facts. Their musings were interrupted by a noise from outside; the sound of a door rattling against a desk.

"We need to move," urged Tabbs. The papers fluttered to the floor as they grabbed Gem and moved quickly out of the office towards the far end of the corridor. They glanced briefly into the rooms on each side. One looked like some kind of operating theatre, though the furniture within had been overturned and strewn around the room. Another room was bare except for a rectangular space in the centre of the floor.

Jon risked a quick peek in, the torchlight revealing an almost empty pool. There looked to be a few feet of what smelled like salt water in the bottom, though it was hard to tell above that terrible odour, overpoweringly strong here once again.

Behind them, the rattling grew more urgent. They flew onwards, plunging down another set of narrow steps, in despair at seemingly going deeper into the complex. The corridor they now moved through was barely six feet wide and carried more ductwork and piping. The only light was from their torches and the faint odour of seaweed and rot grew stronger. They came to a T-junction.

"Which way, which way?" Jon looked left and right in desperation. A distant clatter echoed along the dark corridor behind them. Gem sobbed and Jon put a comforting arm around her shoulders.

"It's okay Gem, we'll get out, I promise. Let's look up here." He started along the left hand passageway, leading Gem with him. Tabbs hesitated as the torch in her hand flickered. She knocked it once, twice, the beam playing back along the corridor. It's light was reflected in two pale orbs shining out of the dark. With a slithering sound, they disappeared quickly. Gasping in fear, Tabbs took a couple of steps back then blindly turned and ran along the right hand passageway.

Jon and Gem meanwhile had run into a closed door at the end of their corridor. Not as large as the entrance doors but steel nonetheless, a long-dead CCTV camera fixed above it. Worse was the heavy chain and padlock securing the large bolt-handle. Jon swore, shrugging off his backpack and rummaging frantically inside.

"Come on, come on," he muttered to himself, then gave a

cry of triumph as he pulled a slim bunch of lock picks out of the bag. Fumbling, he began trying each pick in turn, sighing in relief as the third one produced a click. Ripping the padlock clear, Jon tugged on the bolt then pulled hard. The chain clattered to the ground as the door screeched open six inches. A seaweed smell flowed through and over them like a miasma. Jon put his hands through the opening and, grasping the heavy door, pulled with all his strength.

Beside him, Gem screamed as the sound of slapping feet bounced off the walls behind them. She turned and shone her torch full into the face of the nightmare creature. With a hiss it backhanded her, sending the hateful light clattering away. Gem was knocked across the narrow corridor, head impacting the wall with a sickening crunch.

Jon turned to see Gem slumped to the floor, a smear of red tracing her path down the brickwork. Above her loomed the creature, its stench filling Jon's nostrils. Terror lent him strength. Shouting at the top of his voice, he launched himself at the thing, hoping to push it away from his friend. His hands contacted the slimy, scaly skin of the creature but despite putting all his weight behind it, his push barely registered. The creature turned with blinding speed and with one sweep of a webbed, clawed hand, sliced Jon's throat open to the bone. A spray of bright red blood jetted across the wall as Jon staggered back, eyes uncomprehending, as he too slumped to the cold, damp floor.

Tabbs heard the screams and shouts and guessed what might be happening to her friends. She was torn between safety for herself and helping them. Concern won out and she began retracing her steps back towards the T junction. A sound brought her up short, the slapping of bare feet on concrete. Stifling a sob, she glanced around and dove quickly through the nearest doorway. A hurried glance around showed her she was in some kind of maintenance room, with tools and equipment spread around on benches. She turned off her torch and crouched behind a bench. Reaching out in the dark, her fingers closed around a heavy wrench and she slowly lifted it, resting one end on her shoulder.

The room was in total darkness. Tabb's breath sounded like a bellows, her heart a drum; she closed her eyes for a minute and tried to compose herself. A sound snapped her eyes back open... the door was opening. She had an impression of a presence, a vague shape moving in the gloom. The stench of the thing rolled ahead of it. There was the slap of a step on the floor, then another. Could the thing see in the dark? Could it smell her?

Tabbs clutched the wrench tighter as she felt the thing draw near. Judging it was now or never, she sprang up with a heartfelt cry, swinging the heavy wrench with all her might. She was rewarded with a heavy thud and an inhuman croak from the thing but the impact bounced the wrench from her grip and it fell, with a clang, to the floor.

Without pause, Tabbs moved to where she thought the door was. Her instincts proved sound, she passed through the gap and flicked her torch on again, sprinting headlong along the corridor towards her friend. Seconds later she was brought up short by the sight of them, slumped prone and lifeless on the ground. Gem looked as though she were sleeping, the mark on the wall the only sign of her demise. Jon's face was a pale mask, frozen in terror. His clothing was soaked with blood and it formed a congealing scarlet pool around him.

Tearing her eyes from the horrible sight. Tabbs glanced up and saw the open door. Was the thing behind her wounded? Had her blow killed it perhaps? She gave herself a small pause in which to consider but her hopes were shattered by the distant slap-slap of bare feet.

Overcoming her instinct to stay with her friends, even dead as they were, Tabbs squeezed through the narrow gap, desperately removing her rucksack to do so. Once through, she pushed the door shut behind her, hoping it perhaps had some in-built locking mechanism. The torch beam revealed a brickwork passage, similar to the one the other side of the door. But this finished within a few paces, opening into a much older, natural tunnel that looked hewn from the rock and earth itself. The smell of sea and damp was strong but tinged with a freshness that gave Tabbs hope. With a quick glance back at the closed door, she set off with a determined stride.

Time became meaningless to Tabbs as she traversed the tunnel network. Impenetrable darkness lay ahead and behind the small bubble of torch light. Openings to left and right revealed further passages leading off the main tunnel. Some smelt foul and she decided to stick to the main passageway. After a time, she thought she detected a slight upward slope in the floor and the earth underneath grew damp, her feet sinking slightly into it. Further on, water dripped or trickled down the rock walls. Pools of brackish water lay here and there; Tabbs shone her torch into one, sending the blind, wriggling things within into a frenzy.

Once she paused, frozen in fear at what she thought was a soft footstep behind her. She flicked off the torch and crouched against the damp wall, hardly daring to breathe. But the only sound was the steady drip of water from the ceiling. Minutes passed, until Tabbs flicked on the torch again and continued. There was a definite upward slope now and, to her joy, a soft breeze carried the smell of ozone to her nostrils. The tunnel twisted and turned a little and Tabbs finally saw a dim light ahead. Rounding the turn, the passageway opened out into a small cave. The hiss of sea on shingle sounded ahead and the moonlit beach was the most beautiful sight Tabbs had ever seen.

She stumbled out of the opening, crunching away from the low cliff that housed the cave. She was on a small beach, cliffs behind, the silver water stretching away in front of her. The cliffs seemed to enclose the whole bay. Staggering along the shingle, though, Tabbs saw a narrow band of dunes ahead. She headed towards them and on reaching them sank to her knees on the soft grass and sand. Shock finally overcame her and, trembling, she slowly lowered herself to the ground, curling into a foetal position.

A sound woke her and Tabbs opened her eyes into the dazzle of the rising sun. A dark shape was silhouetted in its glare and Tabbs started back with a fright. The figure raised a hand.

"S'alright my love, I ain't going to hurt 'ee. But 'ee can't stay here, this be a private place."

Tabbs drew her legs up under her and stood, unsteadily. Shading her eyes, she saw the figure was a youngish man, dressed in a raggedy old coat and wellington boots. He had simple but kind look about him and spoke in the broadest Norfolk accent she'd ever heard.

"How'd 'ee get here in any case?" the man asked.

Tabbs briefly recounted last night's events, telling of an attack by a madman in the old nuclear bunker. The man squatted in front of her as he listened, scratching his chin and occasionally glancing up the beach at the cave opening.

"There's none come from the bunker for years. Men in uniforms and suits built it. They came and saw us." he told her.

"What did they want?" Tabbs asked.

"Oh I don't remember," answered the man. "It was Mother they spoke to. She knows all what goes on in these parts." His face was lit with a sudden smile. "Mother! I'll take 'ee to Mother, she'll know what to do!"

The man extended a hand and Tabbs reached out and grasped it to help him up. She gave slight gasp as she noticed the webbing between his fingers but if he noticed her reaction, the man didn't show it.

"Come on!" he cried and set off with long strides through the dunes. With a last glance along the empty beach, Tabbs turned and followed.

The man led her through the dunes to a narrow, sandy track. It cut up towards the lowest part of the cliffs, leading to a narrow set of steps, little more than handholds cut into the rock. Without pause, the man leapt up them, Tabbs rushing to keep up. Atop the cliffs lay an area of heath and marsh that stretched as far as the eye could see. The man took another narrow path and beckoned Tabbs to follow.

Within seconds the sound of the sea had disappeared and Tabbs found herself in a murky, humid marsh. Dense vegetation blocked the view to each side and the air was thick with the smell of stagnation and rot. Midges buzzed incessantly around her head and she made a vain attempt to swat them away. The man bounded on ahead without a backward glance.

After around five minutes, the path opened out into a clearing. The ground here was a little higher, rising towards the centre of the space which was occupied by a tumbledown shack. Tabbs paused, uncertain. The man turned and smiled again.

"S'alright, Mother's inside. This is where she lives now, until it's time to go. Come on in." He turned and opened the creaking door, disappearing inside. Tubbs clenched her fists, sighed and followed him in. The interior was cool and dark. An overpowering odour caused Tabbs to flinch. A sickly, cloying smell that caught in her throat. Something like that time she had visited Gran in the home. But worse, far worse. The man turned.

"Now, Mother's very old, so you'll have to excuse her. Come here so she can see you."

Tabbs shuffled forward into the gloom. Flies buzzed around her. The window in the far wall was largely covered over with old newspaper and in the soft light of an old oil lamp Tabbs could just make out a bulky figure in the bed before her. The figure was swathed in bedclothes and seemed motionless but as Tabbs approached, the figure turned. A hoarse, croaky voice issued from it.

"Well now, who's this? We don't get many visitors here. Come forward, my pretty, let Mother see you."

Hesitantly, Tabbs moved closer, letting out a gasp as Mother's features became clearer. Little was visible above the bedclothes and for that Tabbs was somehow grateful. The eyes drew her attention first. Pale and bulbous, yellowish and milky.

The oddly shaped head was barely covered with sparse strands of lank hair. The skin looked wan and blotchy. And the mouth... Mother's mouth spread wide in a disturbing grin, revealing small triangular, yellowed teeth. The man told how he'd found Tabbs on the beach and she'd come from the bunker.

"Ah, the bunker," Mother wheezed. "Yes, those men from government. They came to us when it was being built, asking all sorts of questions. I told them there's none left of the old families now. But they said they'd found one, a descendant. The fools. I warned them! I told them they couldn't control him once the change started. Once he knew. Oh yes, one of ours he was, young Stephen, not that he knew it." The figure shifted and cackled, a foul waft of breath washing over the mesmerised Tabbs.

"I spoke to him in the way of our kind. In dreams, see? That poor boy, locked away in that horrible place. Oh he found a way out up top eventually. Well he had to eat didn't he, even though our kind can go longer without food than you humans. But he didn't know where he was. Couldn't reach the sea from there, 'specially not in the daylight. But your'n a clever one aren't you? You found a way out. And if you got out to here, reckon as he can too. He's probably on the way now."

Tabbs whimpered and turned to leave but the man moved behind her and firmly grasped her shoulders.

"Now, now, my pretty. Don't be like that. See, I'm far too old now, older than you could imagine. And Stephen Manning was the first new one of our kind round here for many, many years. The rest have all gone, just as my own Mother went, back into the depths."

Tabbs struggled but the man's grip was like iron. Mother

sat up with a groan. Tabbs thought she saw something scuttle across the misshapen face. Mother leaned forward to better view her guest.

"I told the men that *they* were gone now. But I did tell them about the change and how to bring it on. That poor boy, locked away from the sea for so long. But he's free now, you freed him, didn't you, my pretty? And soon he will be here. Back to his own kind. Back to start a new family."

A flock of nearby terns took to the air in response to the scream of despair from the old hut. Then everything was silent in the marsh again, save for the distant sound of slapping feet.

INNSMOUTH ECHOES

DO YOU WANT TO LIVE FOREVER?

Shit, where am I? The back of a limo it seems, must have nodded off. The twinkle of my Nokia woke me, just a text from Momma asking If I'd landed safely. The flight was fine, the Honolulu to Atlanta leg in business class, there's a novelty. From there to Santiago, less comfortable but still okay. Hardly any time to pack or prepare, still that's what happens when you get a summons from one of the world's richest men.

The limo was waiting at the airport, uniformed chauffeur and all. God, I must look a mess. There'd been a couple of calls from the Pierson Broadcasting Syndicate to the office, Judy had passed them on but I ignored them. Calls from media companies are usually because they want a talking head to do a piece on some bullshit news show. I get a lot of that, being "The Dolphin Lady". A bullshit title but it can sometimes help with funding. And, Lord knows, funding is what we need right now.

Our Pacific Whale Foundation funding was drawing to an end and we'd just got the news that it won't be renewed. It was just after that conversation that Judy patched through the call from a Mr Channing Saunders, personal assistant to Mr Michael

Pierson. Well, you don't ignore a call like that. If the founder of PBS wants to talk, then you listen... especially if you need funding. After all the team's work, I'll be damned to let our project go *pau*, not when we are making such breakthroughs in Cetacean communication.

The limo glides to a stop and my driver jumps out to open the door for me, very nice. I see we are at a small harbour, colourful buildings overlooking us from the hills behind. A voice says, "Welcome to the Jewel of the Pacific, Miss Lee," and I turn to see a man in his mid-30's, smart but casual. I'd call his look "preppy"; expensive slip-ons, no socks, tan chinos and a light blue button-down shirt, complete with cravat. Designer shades pushed back onto his blonde-streaked hair, nice green eyes. He walks forward and offers a hand. I feel like a hobo, dressed as I am in Daffy Duck t-shirt, board-shorts and flip-flops. I accept his handshake.

"Channing Saunders, we spoke on the phone. I hope the flight was pleasant, Miss Lee?"

He has a strong Boston accent, with that odd vowel sound.

"Thanks you. Yes, it was. Nice to meet you. And please, call me Mae."

"Very well, Mae, if you'd like to follow me. We don't like to keep Mr Pierson waiting."

Plane, limo, now a luxury boat. I'm going up in the world. The chauffeur carries my luggage aboard and soon we are heading out into the blue waters of the Pacific, as beautiful here as it is back home in Wailuaiki Bay. And for me, the Pacific is a kind of home. I grew up and have worked in and around it all my life.

We head north, I take the chance to enjoy the sun on my

face and the fresh air after spending more than twenty four hours in an air-conditioned metal tube. Half an hour later, we draw in to a small cove, a narrow strip of beach hemmed in by forest. The boat makes for a jetty, beyond which I can see a low, squat building poking out from the tree line. Two locals stand at the jetty, one moors the boat, the other helps me ashore and takes my luggage. I follow him and Saunders towards the building, trying to pretend that this is the kind of thing I do every day.

Closer, it looks to be a single story high. It reminds me of one of those "houses from the future" you used to see in books as kids. The entrance is under a low curved roof, filled with tinted glass. A doorway slides open in the black screen and a maid ushers us inside. The interior is cool, air conditioned, and furnished in minimalist style; just a few expensive objets d'art, a low couch, and a reception desk off to one side. Saunders strides through without acknowledging any of the staff, beckoning me to follow. I nod to the maid and thank the man carrying my bags and follow, along the length of a small corridor, to where he opens a door, telling me. "This is your room. You have a few minutes to freshen up, then I'll take you to meet Mr Pierson." My cases are deposited just inside the door and I'm left alone.

The room is nice, if a bit sparse. A double bed, a desk and chair, an en-suite bathroom. A flat screen TV hangs on one wall, not seen one of those before. Anyway, no time for that, I'd best get changed so I look something like the professional marine scientist I'm supposed to be. I catch myself in the mirror as I wash. Mid 30s, still got a good figure, thanks to all that swimming. My Asian-Hawaiian heritage shows in my golden skin tone and jet black, straight hair. No jewellery save a shark-tooth pendant. Still no engagement or even wedding ring, much to Momma's chagrin. "About time you got a man!" she tells me almost every time we speak. But work comes first and there's been no one prepared to deal with that. Sure, Ben, back at the office has made a few overtures, but mixing work and pleasure is a sure recipe for disaster.

But, anyway, as for now.....wow...all this! *Take a few deep breaths, Mae, try and relax.* After all, Pierson has summoned me so he obviously wants something from me. Therefore, in theory, I'm in the driving seat. Not that it feels like it...

A tap on the door makes me hurry to finish dressing. That's better. In black jeans and crisp, white blouse, I follow the maid back along the corridor and into a small waiting room. She asks permission to search me for any electronic devices, then gets me to sign a non-disclosure form. Still in something of a daze, I scan it quickly and put my mark at the bottom of the page. After that, she leads me into a board room, where five people sit round a large mahogany table. All save one rise as I enter. Saunders steps forward, "Ah, Miss Lee, let me introduce you."

He gently takes my elbow and steers me to the man at the head of the table. It was only as we draw closer that I recognise him - Michael Pierson, owner of one of the largest media companies in the world. From virtually nothing in his native Australia, he has built up an empire of newspaper groups, TV stations and telecoms companies that span the world. Last time I'd seen him on TV, he looked like a spry 70 year old, brusque and abrupt with the interviewer.

The figure in the chair looks at least ten years older. A palsied hand grasps the ivory handle of a walking stick, the face is lined and drawn with pain. But there's no mistaking the steel in the eyes and the harshness of the voice.

"Miss Lee, a pleasure to meet you. Forgive me not standing, my legs don't work so well these days."

I'm not sure whether to bow, curtsey or shake hands. So I settle for a simple, "Thanks you, Mr Pierson, it's nice to meet you to."

Pierson grunts. "Call me Mike, please. Now, let's all sit down, shall we, and I'll tell you what's going on."

I sit at the chair to the right of Pierson and glance around the table as he introduces the others.

"Saunders, my PA, you've already met." Saunders nods. Next to him is a slight man in plain army fatigues, sporting shades, although we are indoors, and a thin, goatee beard. I put him in his fifties.

This is Daniel Warren, Head of Security here at the facility." The man nods impassively.

Next along is a face I recognise. "Dr Jonathan Best," says Pierson. "Marine Biologist."

"We've met," rumbles Jonathan in his rich, Barbadian tone. "The PICES Project, right?"

I nod and smile. "Yes, I remember. How are Marnie and the kids?"

"All fine, all fine." Jonathan grins.

Pierson harrumphs and continues. "And this is Dr Harvey Cottle, geneticist and our Head of Science." Last to be introduced, a large, bald man dressed in a white lab coat. I feel his eyes roam over me as he twirls his pudgy, white fingers and whispers, "A pleasure."

I fix a grin in response and turn back towards Pierson.

"This is very nice, Mr Pierson - erm, Mike - but why am I here?"

"Blunt and to the point, I like it." Pierson gives a smile that doesn't quite reach his eyes. "Very well. You, Miss Lee, are a leading expert in marine communication, correct?"

I stammer, "Well, I suppose, that is -"

"Please, Miss Lee. This is no time for false modesty. Time is one thing I don't have. So let me get straight to the point. I've heard you called "the Dolphin Lady." Some say you have a natural gift for communicating with certain types of marine life, right? Well, Miss Lee, we have a certain type of marine life here that I would like you to communicate with. You see? It's all really quite straightforward."

"What is it?" I ask, curiosity piqued. "A dolphin? A whale?"

I pick up on a glance that flashes between the men. Pierson continues, "Not exactly. Though we do have a dolphin here. We have been using it to see if it could communicate with our…. specimen."

"I'm confused. I specialise in marine intelligence, cetaceans in particular. If you have some kind of fish you want me to talk to, I'm afraid I will disappoint you."

"No, not a fish, Miss Lee. Cottle?"

The heavy man fumbles with his pen before speaking. "What if there were other species in the oceans, Miss Lee? Species not yet discovered?"

I place my elbows on the table. "It wouldn't be unusual. New species are being discovered all the time, new worms, new bugs, new fish."

"But," continues Cottle, "What if the new discovery was intelligent. And I mean, *intelligent*. Dolphin intelligent. Perhaps even human intelligent?"

I'm unable to suppress the small laugh that escapes me. "I would say someone has been watching too many science fiction movies. The odds against such a thing are ..."

"Astronomical?" interjects Pierson. "Perhaps. And yet, Miss Lee, that is precisely what we have. An intelligent specimen of a hitherto undiscovered species. Right here. In my facility."

Well it still sounds crazy but I go along with the ride. "And you want me to what? Talk with this...thing?"

Pierson raps the table top. "Precisely! Talk with it, find out where it's from, find it what it is and find out if there are others. But most of all, Miss Lee, find out how it lives so long! Saunders, I think it's time for Miss Lee to see the lab!"

Five minutes later, I find myself in a state-of-the-art marine science lab. On one side of the space is a sunken pool, which Jonathan tells me opens directly into the ocean, protected by a lowered barred gate. Large metal shutters cover almost the whole length of the opposite wall, from ceiling to floor.

I turn at a familiar splashing and clicking to see the head of a dolphin break the surface of the pool. My smile turns to concern; it seems to be in distress, swimming rapidly back and forth, maintaining its upright position. I approach and kneel at the side of the pool, making some clicking sounds and the dolphin responds immediately, swimming towards me, its own clicking raising in intensity and tempo. It fixes its gaze on me and makes several small darting movements in my direction, before turning away and swimming off. It returns and repeats the same procedure three more times.

Pierson, leaning heavily on his stick appears at my side.

"What's it saying, Miss Lee?"

"She. It's a female. She seems to be warning me about something. It's the kind of behaviour dolphins display when a predator is in the area and there are young ones to protect. But she has no young here, I presume, and I cannot see how there would be any predators."

Pierson nods sombrely and bids me follow him over to the shutters. He signals, Cottle presses a button, the shutters start to rise with a low hum. A glass screen is slowly revealed, behind it murky, green-tinged water. It looks to be a huge tank, some ten feet high and thirty feet wide, built into the side of the room. At one side of it stand steps and a gantry, a chain and hook hanging above. I move closer to the glass, straining to see anything, but there is nothing but murk. Behind me, the dolphin redoubles her chittering. I move forward, feeling somehow drawn to the glass, resting a hand on its cool surface as I peer within; still can't see anything. With the speed of an arrow, a large shape suddenly shoots directly at me, impacting the glass with a thud. The movement and noise make me flinch but what I see freezes me on the spot.

Just the other side of the glass, hand pressed in mirror image of my own, is a figure that is at once both human and icthian. The basic humanoid shape is there, the eyes, a snub nose, the mouth... but mixed in, intermingled with other features. Gill slits at the neck, a milky film that occasionally flicks down over the eyes. Sharp, narrow teeth and the hand... webbed and clawed.

I stumble back as the thing vanishes into the murk and end up sitting on the tiled floor, head spinning.

"Yes, that was the reaction most of us had." Jonathan gives a thin smile as he helps me up. "Ugly sonovabitch, isn't it?"

By now, I'm struggling to draw breath and Jonathan assists me to another room, a rest area, and organises a shot of brandy. Pierson perches in the armchair opposite and regards me closely.

"Now do you see, Miss Lee?"

"And that... it is intelligent?"

"Extremely so, we believe."

"But where did you find it?"

"That is a long story, Miss Lee, but I can condense it to this. I am dying. We all are. Despite my wealth, my influence, my power, I can do little to stave off the effects of ageing and nothing to prevent death itself. For years I've had my people conducting research into life extension. I've seen everything, Miss Lee, from Yogis who claimed to be a hundred and fifty to people selling all types of miracle cure and mumbo-jumbo medicine. It was Saunders who came up with our little treasure. He had been following up leads on certain South Sea island cults, whose priests were said to live for centuries. More mumbo-jumbo, you might think, as did I, but it was through the efforts of Saunders, having established contact with one such cult, that we got our specimen. I regret our methods were somewhat crude but I was never one to be hesitant when it comes to a high stakes game."

"That creature was their *priest*?"

"In a manner of speaking, you might call it that. Hence we understand that it is intelligent. We also understand, thanks to Cottles's gene analysis, that the thing is around 450 years old."

"But that's impossible! The only living creatures to reach that age are trees and the like!"

"Nonetheless, there it is. What I need to know now, Miss Lee, is how does it live so long? What is the secret of its longevity? Something in its metabolism? Something we can extract? That is your job. To talk to it, to find the answers to my questions."

"I don't understand, you have all this equipment."

"Oh we have tried everything, believe me. Various scans, X-rays and tests but the results, according to Cottle, have been inconclusive. Saunders suggested the communication angle. He thinks if we can talk to it, it might provide some information we can use."

"I see. I think. But this place, this lair, this creature..."

Pierson chuckles. "Lair? Miss Lee, I'm a businessman, not a Bond villain. You will be well recompensed for your work here. Tell me whatever your funding needs are for your own projects and I will give you five times that amount."

If I thought my head was spinning enough before, it's now revolving even faster.

"But the scientific implications! They are -"

"Irrelevant to me, Miss Lee. As I said, I'm a businessman. This thing interests me for two reasons. One, can it provide the key to my own life extension? Two, if it can, how can I best market that to people in a similar position? Aside from that, I have zero interest."

I guess he sees the anger flare up in my eyes. I've never been someone who's able to control their temper. He pre-empts me. I'm beginning to get the feeling I've been set up from the very start.

"Come now, Miss Lee, each to their own. I know how much your little research project means to you. If it sugars the pill, I'll cut you in on the deal. If money is not your motivation, then think on this. Your own mother is ill and currently in care, correct? Imagine what you could do for her with this knowledge."

There's that flash of anger again. How dare he! "Why you... how did you know that?"

Pierson closes his eyes and sits back in his chair, looking frail. "Miss Lee, it is my business to know many things. Now, I am tired, time is short, can you give me an answer?"

My brain is still whirling as I weigh up both sides of the situation. In the end, scientific curiosity wins out, tinged with concern for Momma. What if Pierson is right? We could be on the verge of a medical breakthrough.

"Alright. I'll do it."

Pierson's frame sags with relief and he places a hand to his temple. "Excellent. I'll have Saunders bring you the paperwork to look over and sign. Welcome to the team, Miss Lee."

The next couple of days are taken up recovering from jet-lag and getting to know my way around the place. Adjoining the main lab are further research rooms, including one with a large chair, complete with ominous looking restraints, at its centre. We each have our own private room, meals are taken in a small canteen, all domestic duties are taken care of by the small group of staff.

I get the distinct impression that the staff are not run of the mill domestics, an impression verified when I hear Warren briefing a couple of them on security matters. Fair play, I figure, makes sense that you'd keep something like this well under wraps until you were ready to reveal it to the world.

Day three, I'm having my second encounter with the creature. I'm standing in front of the large tank again, not so close this time, and have the opportunity to calmly observe the creature and make notes. It's fascinating. It truly seems to be a blend of the piscine and human. Jonathan talks me through the main points of his own research, conducted over the last week or so.

The creature is ectothermic, it's back covered with cosmoid scales, of a type rarely seen in modern marine life. Its dentition comprises pointed lower teeth with triangular upper, not dissimilar in configuration to the Great White. A predator, then. Hands and feet are webbed and clawed. Height wise, it stands at around 1.7 meters, though it is hunched over, especially when out of the water. Oh yes, it's amphibious as well. I'm not sure how that works, just yet. There are obvious gill slits at the neck but no blow hole as with aquatic mammals. Actually, some aspects of its make-up seem more amphibian than fish. Without dissecting it, I imagine, that remains a mystery. Lord knows what effect this will have on evolutionary theory.

What isn't under question is that the creature is intelligent. I ran some basic cognition tests to start and it scored high on everything. I have no doubt it can understand my gestures and the pictures I held up to it. What remains to be seen is how I can directly communicate with it. I know Pierson is after quick results but you can't rush these things. Before communication, you have to develop a connection, a level of rapport.

Day five, I'm a mixture of happy and furious. We tried direct communication today, we let Kai out of the tank. I called him Kai after an ex, he was all bulging eyes and roaming hands, so it seemed appropriate. Anyway, I was elated at the results but furious at how Kai was treated. Warren had full charge of what he termed *prisoner transport*. First stage was for one his team lean over the top of the tank and catch Kai's wrists in pole loops. From there, his arms were raised up and manacles applied. The hook was then attached to the manacles and Kai was winched up and out of the water. He hung there for a second, water streaming down his body, slowly turning, glaring at us.

Then he was brought across, where manacles were attached to his ankles before he was lowered to the floor. Another pole rod was placed around his neck, a very nervous looking guy grasping the other end of it for dear life. Kai stood hunched, dripping on the tiles. Then with a sudden movement, he snapped his jaws towards one of the assistants. For a second those teeth flashed, then the wide mouth clacked shut. Nowhere near the assistant, who jumped back nonetheless with a small scream. Warren immediately reached to his belt and stepped in. Drawing a black cylindrical device, he flicked a switch and jabbed Kai under the ribs. There was a spark and sizzle, Kai falling to the floor with a load croak.

"Drag it up, get it into the chair!" ordered Warren and his minions obeyed. Within seconds, Kai was strapped in the chair, held in place with the thick restraints. So much for rapport!

Nonetheless, the session went remarkably well. I cleared everyone out of the room, though Warren insisted on staying. I had him sit in the corner, out of view of Kai while I ran through my preliminary communication procedures.

So now I'm just writing up the results and there's a knock on the door. It's Jonathan, he just wants to see if I'm okay after this morning and we talk a little about what is going on. Neither of us likes Warren. Come to that neither of us likes Pierson, either, but we both agree, the potential scientific breakthroughs outweigh any reservations we have at the moment. In any case, as well as my "official" notes, I let Jonathan know I'm keeping my own private journal, too. That seems to mollify him and he bids me goodnight.

Day six, the same procedure, this time, thankfully, without the cattle prod. I'm beginning to form an understanding of Kai's croaks and clicks. Using simple pictograms I am building a picture of how his language works. It is easier than dolphins, much of their language is beyond our range of hearing. Kai's chatter appears to have more in common with our human speech. Not that I've forgotten our dolphin friend, I go to see her every day, though it seems she is no longer talking to me. When I approach, she turns away and swims to the opposite corner of the pool, nudging the bars with her nose.

Mind you, I'm the same with Dr Cottle. Aside from where necessary, I avoid him as much as possible, the man gives me the creeps. More welcome is Channing, he is often hovering around, keeping an eye on things, I guess. He has a nice smile. No sign of Pierson and the lack of outside communication is starting to get to me a bit, I'm not even allowed to call Momma from here. Hopefully, we can get a breakthrough soon.

Yes! Two more days and we have it! Clear and coherent communication! I feel I've established a bond with Kai and we are now talking like old friends. Once he is returned back to the tank, none too gently by Warren's people, I ask Channing if I can see Pierson.

Ten minutes later, I'm back in the boardroom, just me, Pierson and Channing. This time I get straight to the point.

"Okay, here it is. The subject is of a race of sea creatures known, as far as is translatable, as *Deep Ones*. They have very little in the way of written history but seem to have been around from the year dot, at least as long as humans, maybe even longer. They are much fewer in number than they were, for many reasons. One is mankind's continued abuse of the sea. Pollution and so on. Two is their breeding cycle. Although they live for a long time, hundreds of years it seems, they rarely breed. I'm a bit unclear about how the breeding takes place, there is a term Kai uses that I am unable to translate."

"Kai?" interjected Pierson.

"Oh, I gave him a name, makes it easier to establish a connection. He told me his real name but I can't pronounce it."

"Give me strength," muttered Pierson. "Alright, continue."

"The longevity seems to be a genetic function, something in the DNA. The interesting thing, according to Dr Cottles's research, is how closely their DNA matches ours. Almost as though we had a common ancestor. In phylogenetic terms - "

Pierson raised a shaky hand. "Miss Lee, if you could skip the big words and just get to the punch-line, I'd appreciate it."

"I'm sorry. Okay, in a nutshell, we can take a fluid sample from Kai that we think could prove the basis of a life extension serum. Kai has confirmed this and given information on how to go about it. Despite their primitive appearance, his people seem to have a highly developed measure of scientific knowledge, at least in the areas of husbandry."

"That's all I needed to know, Miss Lee, thank you. I will get Cottle onto it immediately. Excellent, you've done very well. I will arrange for the transfer of relevant funds to your account and you can be on your way home forthwith."

I mutter a thanks and stand to leave, then pause and turn in the doorway.

"Actually, would it be okay if I stayed a little longer? I'd love to see the results and also think I can communicate further with Kai. It could be helpful to the whole process."

Pierson shrugs. "As you wish, Miss Lee, as you wish."

Next day and I'm beginning to wish I'd taken the offer of the boat out. Cottle is running things now, I'm relegated to waiting around making soothing noises to Kai when he gets agitated. Which is quite frequently at the moment. Despite him having shown no signs of aggression since that first incident, Warren continues to treat Kai like a wild animal. I have tried to explain, Warren just laughs in my face. It was only when Channing intervened that Warren backed down a little. I thanked him with a small peck on the cheek.

But right now I'm sitting here wringing my hands as Cottle works to get the first sample. It's a painful procedure, he has to go into the spinal column. This involves Kai being restrained while the syringe is pushed slowly into his lower back. I guess anyone who's had a lumbar puncture will know how that feels. The difficulty of procedure is exacerbated by Kai's tough, scaly hide, some of which Cottle has had to cut away. Added to that, he didn't want to chance anaesthetic, not knowing how our patient's system may react, so Kai is undergoing the full agony of the procedure with no pain relief at all.

It's upsetting to see him writhe, the muscles on his arms and legs knotting as he struggles against the restraints. Even worse, his eyes were fixed directly on mine the whole time. He understands what is happening and what is brave is that he consented to it. Though I suspect, consent or not, the procedure would have gone ahead anyway. I soothe him with words as best I can before his limp form is returned once more to the water. There, at least, he seems to revive a little.

Three times the procedure has been repeated now, I swear Cottle is taking some form of pleasure from it. He knows I have a bond with Kai, perhaps this is his twisted way of punishing me for rejecting his all too obvious advances. Jonathan has left already, his work on the project complete. I was sad to see him go, even a little jealous that he has got to escape, but then I remembered I volunteered to stay. Glad that I did in a way, as I was telling Channing over dinner last night.

Today, Cottle finally has his serum ready and will be injecting Pierson, who has refused any tests on others, he feels there is no time to waste. In his words the serum will either work or it will kill him. I'm not let into the med bay while that procedure is being carried out, so I'm waiting in the main lab, talking to Kai through the glass. My dolphin lady still ignores me, Kai has told me his kind do not get on well with the dolphins, though he hasn't explained why.

Thinking about it, seeing the dolphin sad and penned, leads me to make a decision. As she no longer has apart to play in the research, I open the gate and release her back into the sea. Before leaving, she turns, making more sounds, thanks or warning I don't know. Then she disappears into the blue.

With nothing else to do I spend a little time sunbathing outside, then go to the canteen for some dinner. Channing walks in and sits opposite as I am finishing, beaming.

"It's taken! Looks like it's going to work!

I place my hand on his across the table. "That's great news!

So what happens now?"

"Now we can prepare for the next stage. This place can be shut down and we move on to Phase Two. What about you?"

I'm pleased to note he hasn't moved his hand.

"Back to Hawaii, I guess to complete my research project. Also let Momma know the good news, that there may be something that can help her condition."

"That's nice. Though if you ever fancied travelling..."

The rest of the sentence goes unsaid as Cottle comes into the canteen, a sneer on his face as he sees us together. He storms over to the table.

"If you're not too busy, Saunders, Mr Pierson says we to are instigate shutdown procedure. Immediately!" With that he spins and stomps heavily off.

"What does that mean?" I ask.

"Never you mind," Channing replies. "Listen, get your things packed as quick as you can, the boat will be ready to take you back down the coast soon. I'll radio ahead to organise the car and flights."

Then he stands and leaves. Somewhat confused, I head back to my room and, in a few minutes, am packed. The maid knocks and carries my luggage to reception, I follow, still in a slight daze. *Hold on, I can't leave without saying goodbye to Kai, it doesn't seem right.* Telling the maid I will just be a minute, I turn and hurry back down to the main lab.

I walk in to a tense situation. Channing stands between Warren and the tank. With a gasp I see Warren is holding a rifle! Cottle, stood behind Warren, spins to face me as I enter.

"No! I won't let you!" Channing shouts at Warren.

His reply is a sneer as he pulls back the bolt on the gun.

"I don't care if you'll let me or not, smart boy. I'm under orders to tidy this place up. That means leaving no evidence. And that means disposing of this animal!"

"What on earth are you doing?" I cry. "Cottle, how can you agree to this?"

"Simple, Miss Lee," he smirks. "Pierson pays me well. We have enough samples from your fishy friend to synthesise our serum. We can't take the risk of anyone else getting hold of our specimen, the most sensible and safest thing to do is terminate it. I'm looking forward to the dissection!"

I shout and move towards Warren but Cottle is quicker, surprisingly fast for a man of his build. In three steps he is in front of me, slapping me hard across the face. I'm stunned, half turned and feel his arms close around me, grasping me tight, as he snarls, "Do your job, Warren, I'll take care of this bitch!"

Channing steps forward, hands raised, Warren lifts the gun and clubs him hard with the butt. Horrified, I see Channing slump to the tiles, blood already oozing from a gash on his forehead. Warren nimbly runs up the steps at the side of the tank, taking up position on the gantry, pointing the rifle into the water.

"Now, you slimy motherfucker. Where are you?"

The response is a geyser of water as Kai surges a full three meters out of the tank, bursting from the surface with a guttural cry. Before Warren can respond, two large webbed hands are clasped around the back of his head and Kai falls back, taking Warren with him, the rifle clattering uselessly down the steps to the floor.

"Warren! Warren!" shouts Cottle, slightly loosening his grip on me. It's all I need. I throw my head back, feeling the sharp impact against his nose. Straight away, I wrench his thumb, releasing the grip, then spin and hit him as hard as I can in the belly. He stumbles and I rush over to Channing, who is now on all fours, dazedly shaking his head. I quickly help him up and turn, to see Cottle scuttle across the tiles. He heads straight for the rifle, picking it up in clumsy hands, blood pouring from his nose. His face is a mask of pure hate as he levels the barrel.

"Fuck you!" he screams, fiddling with the gun as he stands before us. Behind him in the tank, a figure looms on the other side of the tank, then disappears.

"Warren! Warren!" Cottle shouts, catching a glimpse, perhaps, of the shadow behind him. Channing laughs, wiping the blood from his eye. "You fool. Warren is dead. And so are you!"

There is an explosion of glass as Kai launches himself through the side of the tank like a battering ram. Riding the swell of water that bursts forth, he cannons into Cottle, knocking him to the floor.

Kai's jaws open wide, I am mercifully spared the sight of what happens next as both are submerged in the frothing water. The green, tinged with red, sweeps over us and we are both knocked back towards the pool. Channing grabs me, whispers, "Trust me!" And plunges us into the cool water. I barely have time to take a quick breath before we dive into the depths. Channing, one arm around my waist, strikes out with his other hand, pausing only to pull away the cravat at his neck.

To my shock I see gill slits there, rippling in the soft light. With powerful strokes, he takes us down and through the open gate, out into the ocean beyond. My pulse is pounding and black spots swim before my eyes as I see the sunlight dappling through the water above. Seconds later, we burst up to the surface and, as I cough and splutter, Channing gently carries me to the shore.

On the warm sand, on all fours, I cough a little more before recovering. Channing sits and waits, eyeing me with an amused grin. The sound of a helicopter breaks the silence, lifting from somewhere above the trees behind us and speeding away inland.

"Ah, there goes Pierson." Channing says.

I'm barely capable of any speech beyond, "What the fuck..."

"I owe you an explanation," he replies. "Now that the mission has been successful, I can tell you. For even if you tell others, no one will believe you."

"I don't understand. Mission? Are you a spy or something?"

"Of a sort. My real name is not Saunders, it is Marsh. I come from an old New England family. Old money, you might say, very old money. Our people have had a long affinity with our cousins from the deep, though for decades we have been struggling. Mankind." He scowled. "A blight on the land and now a blight on the sea, too. The time has come for change. We are approaching a new millennium, in more ways than one."

"But what...? I still don't get it?"

"I was sent out, Mae, to become close to Pierson. My sister Sonia and I, the only young ones within our community, were both sent out to learn the modern ways, in order to prepare our people. It took me years to work into my position with Pierson but those we serve do not think in years, not even decades. They think in centuries."

"And what was your mission?"

"We knew Pierson was interested in life extension. It was

a simple thing to bring him one of our own cousins. To let him think he had made this discovery."

"Kai?"

"Yes, though that is not how we know him. A brave volunteer, for he knew the hardships he would have to undergo."

"But why? All this just to make Pierson live longer?"

Channing laughs. "Not entirely, though that is a side effect. No, we wanted Pierson to undergo the *change*. To become one of us. That process is now under way."

"But he has escaped, I take it that was him in the helicopter?"

"Yes, it was. It doesn't matter that he has gone. Once you undergo the change there is no escape from the call. He will return to us, as one of us. And when he does, we shall have control of his media empire."

"Why would you need that?"

"Because as I said, dearest Mae, a new millennium is approaching. Not your trivial human Y2K but something much more significant. The stars will soon be right! Those of us above must prepare the way for those to come."

"But what about Cottle, the science, the discoveries?"

He gave me a sad smile. "He proved useless. Cottle was like a monkey trying to work a computer. We had hopes but it became apparent that he would make no discoveries, not even those we wished him too."

"And all my work, the communication?"

"A sham too, I'm afraid. We needed a credible channel to convince Pierson to take the injection. Cottle would have been groping for months, even years, before discovering what you told him."

"Then I was set up too?" I feel my fists clench.

"I'm afraid so, Mae. But look!" He glances over my shoulder. "Look, out there!"

I follow his pointing hand to see a dark shape bobbing out in the swell. It raises a webbed hand before disappearing below the waves.

"Even now he goes to spread the news to his kin. They will be preparing for the event to come, when the tides will rise and we spill forth in the Great Surfacing!"

I struggle to take all this in, my mind a maelstrom of fears and emotions. "And me," I eventually squeak. "What about me, now?"

Channing puts an arm around me and draws me close. He whispers in my ear. "You just have one question to answer, Mae Lee. Do you want to live forever?"

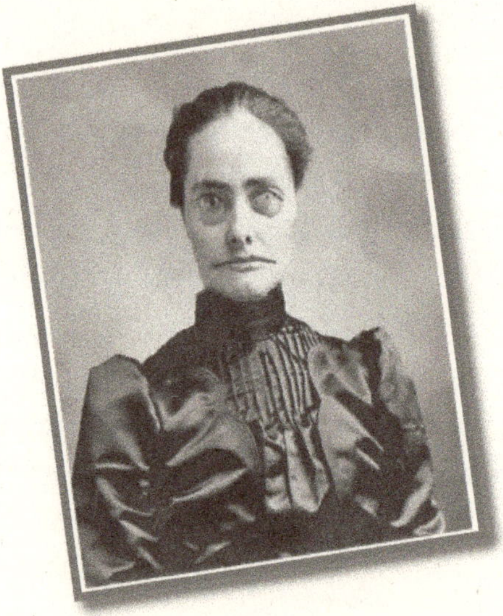

VOSTOCK 5

"Yuri, can you hear me? This is Sergei, come in. Yuri? Yuri, can you hear me? Shit."

STATIC

"This is Vostock Five Antarctic Research Centre, is anyone receiving, over? I repeat again this is Vostock Five Antarctic Research Centre, my name is Professor Sergei Krasilchik. It is 08.30 hours local time, 15th April 2023. Is anyone receiving over?"

STATIC

"This is Vostock Five Antarctic Research Centre is anyone receiving, over?"

STATIC

"Yuri, I'm back on your frequency again. Are you receiving? Please respond! Yuri, I don't know what's happening. There's been no communications for two days now and the team hasn't returned. I'm on my own here at the station, am in lockdown at the moment. There's a ferocious blizzard outside, it came in last night, the readings are off the scale The wind is howling like a mad thing. Yuri, are you there?"

STATIC

"Shit, what was that! Hang on, Yuri, I'll be back in a second."

STATIC

"It's okay, just the wind banging some equipment round outside. I've never known it this bad before. Anyway, like I said, the team have not returned. They went out nine days ago after we sighted those strange lights. Bright violet orbs, they rose slowly above the mountains then shot up into the sky. Quite a beautiful sight, really, though I find those mountains ominous. Sounds mad, doesn't it? Me, the great explorer, worked on expeditions all over the world, acting like a frightened child at the sight of some mountains. But they do look odd. Perhaps it's just the environment, I've been on Polar expeditions before but never this far in. There is a certain kind of splendid desolation here, it's easy to imagine I'm the only person on the planet. One second, Yuri, I'm just going to scan the frequencies again."

STATIC

"Still nothing. Must be the blizzard. So, yes the team set out to investigate. Not just the lights, there was the rumbling too. I've heard glaciers breaking before, you know how that sounds, it's like thunder. This was similar but deeper, much deeper. You could feel it in your bones. I swear the station shook and the lights flickered. Professor Ozero, our geologist, posited it might be an earthquake, though the instrument readings were like nothing he'd seen before. Imagine that, Yuri, we could have discovered some new natural phenomena! Anyway, Danshov decided to take the team out to investigate, so off the four of them went. I drew the short straw and got to stay in the warm. Thank God, with this blizzard. I'm sure they will be okay out there, it's a few days to the mountains but they have good equipment and gear with them. I imagine they are holed up somewhere until this damn storm passes. Okay Yuri, time for another scan."

STATIC

"Still nothing. This must be a hell of a storm to affect even our satellite comms. I can't hear you, Yuri, I hope you can hear me, though. Anyway, where was I. Ah yes, the lights and rumbling. Well that wasn't the only strange thing, we've been getting all the reports of the floods, of course. Sounds like you guys are having a rough time of it. I heard St Petersburg got hit hard, so hope you guys at the AARI are all okay. There's been nothing on the news channels since, well we've not been getting any transmissions on anything the last few days. The last comms that did come through was an odd one. It was from Moscow, came through on vid-link, a crazy looking guy screaming about "things in the river." Maybe I picked up a clip from some crappy old sci fi movie, none of it made sense. Anyway, he ranted on for a bit about "they are coming out of the river!" then the signal dropped. At least up here I am safe from the crazies, eh Yuri? Hang on. I'm going to scan again"

STATIC

"Sorry, Yuri, I just made myself a coffee and some soup. Where was I? Oh yeah, so before the team left we were watching the news reports about the floods. One of those "perfect storm" things, from the looks of it. I didn't bother watching after the team had left, just listened to my music. It's great being here alone, I can turn the music up as loud as I like, I reckon I'm the only Motorhead fan on the continent! I'm just going to see if I can raise the team, back in a minute."

STATIC

"No, still nothing on the local LMR system either. Damn storm. I hope they are okay. I hope my family are okay, too. Yuri, can you do me a favour? Can you call Olyesa, just check that she is okay? I mean I know they are miles from the sea in Voronezh but if you could check that would great. I did try calling on the IP phone, but nothing. Little Sasha starts school this year, they grow so fast! And do say hello to your mother for me, Yuri, I hope she is feeling better. Shit! One second, Yuri."

STATIC

"Back again. The lights went out. Just checked the generator, don't know what happened. Looks like some kind of power surge but where that came from I have no idea. Anyway I've lit a candle and am waiting for the reserve generator to kick in. I hope it does soon, it's minus 55 outside, hey that makes even St Petersburg look warm, eh, Yuri? Luckily this radio set has its own batteries, so I'm still good to talk. Hold on. I'm just going to try and raise the team again."

STATIC

"Still nothing. Well I can't do anything until this blizzard blows over, all I can do is sit tight. So it's just me, my candle and Motorhead sitting here at the bottom of the world. I do hope you are there, Yuri. Can you hear me? Yuri?"

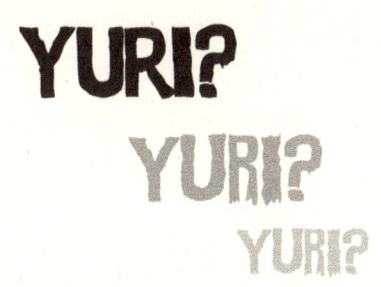

Yuri?

YURI?

YURI?

YURI?

YURI?

YURI?

INNSMOUTH ECHOES

With thanks to Robert Lloyd Parry

www.nunkie.co.uk

for use of "Fear at the Fitz" title

Check out his fantastic tours and readings!

If you have enjoyed this book,
please post us a review on
Amazon. Thanks!

www.innsmouthgold.com

THE DUNWICH TRILOGY

A MODERN MYTHOS TRILOGY!
Based around the crumbling seaport on England's desolate East Coast, this modern take on Lovecraft's classic *The Dunwich Horror* sees unsuspecting people wrestling with the horrors of the Cthulhu Mythos!

THE DUNWICH NIGHTMARE
DC Marcus Hinds and journalist Suzy Bainbridge get drawn into a mystery following a series of grisly murders at Dunwich. Could there be a connection to the nearby top secret research facility?

THE DUNWICH CRISIS
The scale of the conspiracy is revealed as Marcus and Suzy are drawn deeper into the nightmare. Meanwhile an ancient evil stirs in the depths of the North Sea and the world is about to change forever!

THE DUNWICH LEGACY
The true purpose of the Geneva CERN facility is revealed and Marcus plunges into the "world beyond" in order to save his friends and avert global catastrophe.

OUT NOW!
In paperback, e-book or PDF download.
Available via Amazon or direct from
www.innsmouthgold,.com

Printed in February 2023
by Rotomail Italia S.p.A., Vignate (MI) - Italy